Reema Moudgil is an artior over
fifteen years, has writte...rt, travel
and architecture.

PERFECT EIGHT

Reema Moudgil

TRANQUEBAR

TRANQUEBAR PRESS
An imprint of westland ltd
Venkat Towers, 165, P.H.Road, opp. Maduravoyal Municipal office, Chennai 600 095
No.38/10 (New No.5), Raghava Nagar, New Timber Yard Layout, Bangalore 560 026
Survey No. A-9, II Floor, Moula Ali Industrial Area, Moula Ali, Hyderabad 500 040
Plot No 102, Marol Coop Ind Estate, Marol, Andheri East, Mumbai 400 059
47, Brij Mohan Road, Daryaganj, New Delhi 110 002

First published in India by TRANQUEBAR PRESS 2010

ISBN: 978-93-80032-87-0

This book is a work of fiction and any resemblance to people living or dead is
incidental. The places mentioned in the book are occasionally real and partly amalgamate
many places.

Typeset in Sabon Roman by SÜRYA, New Delhi
Printed at Thomson Press India Ltd.

For J.N. Sharma . . .

For teaching sunshine in all weathers.
For translating the tardy rumble of a train to, 'kabhi toh pahunch hi jayenge' (some day we will reach where we must). Thank you for bringing me this far . . .

And Sunita Sharma for hot tiffins, dance costumes made out of sarees, perfectly creased school uniforms, order and comfort in a chaotic world.

1

IN MISSAMARI'S CANTONMENT, the sun grew wistful and grazed windows like an overripe orange itching to be picked. In the evening, it melted away like a pale, hard-boiled candy on windowpanes, willing me to brush my fingers against it before it was all gone.

Neither imperfections, nor change had any place within Missamari. At night, watchful fire-torches held up by invisible hands guarded it; in the morning, its fenced and barbed boundary walls shut out civilian gaucherie, unmet needs, disorder and chaos. Nothing could alter its rhythm or shatter its poise. Not wars. Not mosquitoes. Not lizards that went kit . . . kit . . . kit during hot summer nights. Not the domestic squabble that once erupted in an officer's home and resulted in a kitchen fire which many believed was started by the wife herself to melt her anger in.

Missamari did not flinch or mope when its men faced bullets during wars or when a young soldier died of tapeworm during peace. Grief, when it arrived, was cast aside because it came in the way of life. The cantonment took pride in its health. In its square-shouldered officers. In regularly pruned trees with trunks that were numbered and banded with white paint. In buildings unchipped by age and untouched by seasons.

Monsoon was dismissed with indulgent smiles even as rains pounded doors with angry fists, flooded hollows, pulped distant foothills and tore clouds in futile anger. Army wives piled up bravely in splashy jongas and headed towards tarpaulin-coated, shivering Sunday marts, where they picked up saree hems, ducked showers and bought black-seeded, cardamom bananas, rain-salted fish and the oozing joy of overripe pineapples. As the jeeps veered back to the cantonment, toothy tires rutted the mud, bamboo groves winked and hummed in the rain.

But no rain could seep into the crisp, happy, white-washed cores of army homes where ovens grew warm, rain songs crackled out of radios and children snuggled under yellow, ribbed Assamese quilts. No one ever acknowledged snakes, because broom-wielding orderlies shooed away the foolish, limp things when they sneaked into toilet bowls or festooned curtain rods. And if one unthinkingly wound its way into the Army School, the tribal watchman scanning the compound bounded after it, humoured it for some time, let it thrash, arch, vault over puddles. And then pierced its fear-crazed length with a spear, held it up to amuse squealing children, put the limp garland around his neck and danced a jovial tandav like Shiva. At dusk, he roasted and ate his prey with toddy-thickened friends.

When the rain became just a beady fringe around the trees, the sun exploded in the sky, turning Missamari into a bright, crayon drawing. Children tumbled out of homes to reclaim their front-yards. I often saw Ma looking at them, with a sad, half-finished smile. As if they had something she had either lost or misplaced somewhere. I never saw her smile too much. Life for her was a puzzle halved into life and death, and she had never been able to decide which piece she wanted.

I learnt from her to smell grief before it struck. To turn foreboding into a fine-tuned instrument. Just a day before the Big Fete, when the school sky was littered with balloons and silver stars, I announced, 'It will all go waste, Ma. It will rain tomorrow.'

Monsoon was officially over, but it rained. And even though I had known it all beforehand, I could not bear to see the limp festoons. Or the gauzy triangles and furling red, paper snakes dying prematurely in mud. I knew, however, that they had to die. Because everything died. Beautiful things. Loved things. It was risky to love anything too much. And silly to take anything for granted.

Even the Officers' Mess, with its equanimity of luxury, good manners and fearless happiness, could not lull me into contentment.

'*Labalab hai kahin sagar, kahin khali piyale hain, ye kaisa daur hai saki, ye kya taksim hai saki?*' sang Papu one evening in the Mess, closed eyes trying to recall his favourite Kaifi Azmi nazm, when I interrupted a brood of gently-rouged women daintily sipping their lime juice cordials. When they all turned to me, glossy mouths parted in indulgent smiles, I said, 'Did you hear, a poor jawan recently died of a tapeworm? What does a tapeworm look like, aunty? Does it grow into a long snake and curl and uncurl inside someone before killing them?'

The sullen silence they answered me with grew thick and dark when, a week later, at a children's party, I cornered the mother of the drooling birthday girl and asked, 'Aunty, do you remember Mrs Vasanth, our neighbour who set herself on fire? Do you know that she then hid herself in her bathroom because she could not bear to be seen without her skin?'

The cantonment clammed up against me. And since I did not mispronounce words or lisp through a baby mouth, adults stopped pinching my cheeks or pulling my pigtails.

Ma and Papu never told me that I was strange because I chewed the perfect white of NP chewing gum with an almost vengeful anger. Or because I never let beautiful things be and even bled my vegetable-dyed wooden blocks to a muddy ugliness in a water tub. They only scolded me when I padded into the orderly's lime-washed room, opened his Champa hair oil bottle and emptied his Ponds talcum powder jar. They asked me, but I could not explain why I had enjoyed pouring the oil till its ruby-red, ribbony haze had joined the talcum powder mound on the floor, forming a viscous red and white puddle near my feet. That looking at that puddle made me think that, in life, wrong things always got mixed up and nothing was sealed against damage.

Sometimes, without telling Ma and Papu, I went past the sacred cantonment grass and climbed over the barbed boundary walls to explore the other half of humanity in Missamari. Once I found a few smudged children digging the earth deep with their fingers to get to the fat toes of sweet potatoes. They befriended me after I gave them a small blade to help them along. They began to smile hesitantly at me and to wistfully run their dark, bright, hungry eyes over my flowered frock, my neat ponytail. I wished they knew they had nothing to fear from me. I wished I could tell them that I was no different from them. That Missamari's air pulsing with soft, mellow miracles was not mine. Nor Ma's.

I wished I could tell them that nothing was permanent for us. Happiness was something we would always leave behind and go somewhere else.

2

MA, HOWEVER, FOUND ways to trap joy in little crevices of her life. She filled our balcony with baby roses. She made a long duster for the green flowered sofas. She was particularly fussy about her plastic animal-paper grass zoo and her wide-eyed Assamese dolls shuttered behind the glass showcase that I shattered one day, when I threw something sharp and cruel against it. It was on the day Sunny's mother visited us. From my balcony, I often watched her bright green and yellow lawn where she daily offered her son's stricken leg like a stoic prayer to the sun. Sunny had a bad leg, a leg that uselessly dragged after him. Every afternoon, his mother traced a route of faith from calf to knee, willing the bad to turn into good. Tapping, kneading and knuckling the futility congealed in the sad baby leg cursed by the gene gods. The leg often invited perfumed whispers in the Officers' Mess to roost upon it. Rumour had it that Sunny's parents were first cousins and he was the misshapen fruit of their shameful lust.

Sunny was my twin scar and we smelt each other's lacks

and bonded during a safari to the Kazirunga National Park. Because he could not walk too much, we had stayed together in a jeep to watch multilayered rhinos lumber around with their single horns that shone like trophies on happy days and turned into death warrants on bad ones when poachers got lucky. Sunny had put a fat forefinger in a seed-shaped nostril and said, 'God loves me but he can't help much. He is upstairs and I am downstairs. I can't climb up and he can't get down.'

We had then crouched companionably behind tall, bamboo grass to watch an elephant family drinking from a small lake. And we had clutched each other in fear when a swollen elephant mother had cried for help. In an instant, gnarled elephant midwives had surrounded her. Before the baby elephant could arrive in that sacred circle, we left for home.

Sunny talked all the way back, making up for his quiet leg. He told me many stories, like the one about his trip to a tribal temple.

'The temple was in the jungle. It was big and grey. With tall trees all round. Like an elephant hiding in tall bushes. Some people were killing goats in the front yard. They were supposed to be given away to the Gods though I could not understand why the Gods needed dead and not living goats. Ma didn't let me see much but I saw something. A goat with white eyes, a white foaming mouth. Just when the knife cut its throat, the poor goat ran down a hill. Without its neck. It ran down! This poor goat with no head! Then the legs remembered that they were running without a neck so they stopped and the goat fell down dead.'

We became best friends and because we were neighbours, we remained so.

Superman being out of his league, Sunny was content to playact as a turtle and often made his orderly Radhe Shyam tie a basket on his back and mine to have a turtle race. Whenever we crawled together, I told him all my secrets between our synchronised huffs, 'I had ... huh ... curls and pink cheeks ... huh ... when I was a baby. But when I grew up ... huh ... huh ... I became ... huh ... ugly.'

When we stopped, I showed him the dark shadows under my eyes. My straight, damp, black and brown hair. My brown, opaque skin. My sad, wet eyes. My constant frown. Sunny nodded in grief. He knew all about the dark shadows of misfortune. He felt different too, because of his leg. A leg that would obey no command, not even his shrill mother who constantly said, 'Baby, you have a bad leg but it will improve.'

Sunny told me he often heard her voice even in his dreams. I didn't like his mother. She did not understand what Sunny's leg felt from inside; and she always walked into our gentle turtle universe—to disrupt us, ignore me, untie Sunny's hump, and carry him to her perfect dahlia patches. To avenge Sunny, I told her once, 'Aunty, you have one nose, two eyes and a mouth, but something's missing. But you will improve too—just like Sunny's leg.'

I disliked her even more when she came home one day to visit Ma.

She looked around our drawing room, wrung her thin hands till they disappeared in a brown whirl and told Ma, 'Your green curtains are lovely Mrs Sharma. Mine are peach, did you notice? I got them from Panipat. My sister sent me. Now can you give me that cake recipe?'

Ma smiled at her and opened her recipe book. As the

backlit green curtains rested quietly on the windows, Ma lined a squatty tin (a full-grown ghee canister in a previous life and still smelling of animal fat) with a large paper moon cut out of *Filmfare*, and poured the fruit cake batter in it. The two women nodded with approval at each other. Slowly, the cake began to brown upon super-star Rajesh Khanna's smiling face, the fan began to dispense vanilla vapours and the house began to smell of walnuts and chopped glazed fruit. Both women sighed happily and their clinking needles began to knit together a placid, unthreatening day.

It was then that I screamed. And threw something at the showcase glass protecting plastic animals (free with every Binaca toothpaste tube) on paper grass, looking up at pretty dolls.

I heard Ma's voice tight with reigned in panic, 'Are you hurt? Stay where you are ... there's a glass piece next to your right foot! And why are you not wearing chappals?'

'She's not normal,' said Sunny's mother, as she transmitted shudders next to the slivered showcase. 'Please don't mind but she's not like ... a child,' she swayed on her feet and told the jagged glass.

I understood the anger. She didn't like me. But her words fitted into the hollow, jigsaw puzzle I carried within myself. Small, pert explosions went off in my head. And I hopped and screamed around myself in happy recognition.

That was it. I was not like any child I had known. I was a little like Sunny. My legs could go anywhere they wished but my soul could not. It was paralysed.

The fact that I was dysfunctional was now an established fact—just like the cake which had now been loosened with a serrated knife and upturned on a tray. And as with Sunny, my dysfunction was also gene-deep. What a mess it all was. And all because Ma had jumped from a second-floor window when she was six.

3

MA HAD SEALED her fate and mine against joy the day she chose to jump from a window ledge. No one had known what storms had been gathering within her that day.

Before she jumped, she had told herself, 'It does not matter one way or the other.' She jumped because she believed it was futile to hold on to any ledge in life.

But she got something wrong because she floated down safely, thanks to her blue frock that sprouted like a benign parachute well in time.

Everyone wondered how she had escaped with just a few bruises.

She wondered too. And then went on to embrace more injuries, jumping again and again, from other windows and other ledges. Denying herself the choice of holding on to life's promises.

She walked into her damp marital home in Patiala with docile vermilion-stained feet, letting darkness seep into her unresisting sponge bones. She lit up hungry, empty rooms like a living fuel. Needed no one to break and forcibly fit her into the hard, chafing contours of her new family. She did all the breaking herself.

She taught herself the skill of stepping over raw nerves and dousing sudden tempers expertly. And learnt her husband's family history but never shared her own.

A few months into her marriage, she decided to go back to her teaching job in a government school in Panjhal, a one-eyed, unblinking Himalayan village where, in the light of oil lanterns, cats flipped and flopped onto mud floors from thatched roofs to lick sleeping babies and their milk bottles.

When she was packing her limp suitcase, Papu's elder brother gave her the documented remains of a failed family business and told her, 'This is a dead snake. It was killed by your husband. I can't carry it around my neck alone.'

Ma memorised the creditors and decided that each month, she would slice her salary in half till all the names on the list were crossed out.

In Panjhal, she discovered that she was pregnant. During the winter holidays, she came back to Papu to nurse her pregnancy. She stayed quiet even through the loss of the unborn son when Papu drove her impulsively on a scooter across a dry riverbed for a doomed picnic.

She spent her recuperation period learning that the children in the house liked sugar with their rice. That no one liked brinjal. And she sat day after day like a penitent prisoner next to a hand-pump with a bone-dry soap to wash piles of clothes.

She did not allow herself any rage when shirts with stained collars, sarees with curry stars and pyjamas with dead sperms were thrown down at her from the first floor of the house.

She extended her vacation. She continued to scrub in a trance.

But one night the trance broke and—not in resignation but in rebellion—she walked out into the night when everyone was asleep and kept walking till she reached a bridge. Then she stood still like a moonlit, blue and silver Buddha. A hollow-eyed Buddha holding a swollen belly.

She watched the black waters below and meditated about death and peace. And freedom from the pain of drawing her breath. From a windowless kitchen and its malfunctioning stove, a body that was once again big with an unloved child and a man who could give passion but not comfort. From the morose Lambretta her husband drove sometimes to a cinema hall, carrying her silent misery and a niece sandwiched between them.

Had she jumped, she would have been spared a lot. Including the lonely prayers she chattered when I fell dangerously sick as a two-month-old baby in Panjhal and she had to tie me to the back of a hefty student and run through the forests to catch the morning bus to the nearest doctor.

Had she taken that final plunge into the darkness, her last sigh would have been one of relief. She would not have blamed anyone. Least of all her husband. She knew by then that he was very good at huge, monumental things like optimism and courage but could not manage the ordinary bits. Just like people who can blast mountains but fumble helplessly with locks and keys.

She tasted death on the tip of her tongue and braced herself. It was when she rose on her toes to jump that I began to stir inside her.

She stopped and listened to me. I grew still too and listened to her. And we both became each other for a long, quiet moment. Life began to seep back into her bones. But the pain did not seep out.

It got mixed up with the fluids around me and within me. She and I held each other like two red-eyed people in a morgue watching their shared history stretched out on an ice slab.

And then we promised each other that we would always hold each other. And would always trust pain more than happiness.

Ma's history and mine too was done to death in Lahore when she was just five. At the exact moment Pakistan was hewn out of India. Till then, Lahore had felt like a quilted cradle in which Ma had slept each night, listening to honeyed lullabies.

Ma's family had owned the largest toy store in town where she spent hours, putting dolls to sleep and waking them up. Her tubbiest baby had a small cot all to himself. The wooden trains did not interest her much but she liked the shining vessels and the tea sets and took them home to cook in and serve her stuffed children.

Kalyani, Ma's mother, had milky-white skin with strands of saffron in it and was considered one of the most beautiful women in Lahore. On festive days, she hand-printed walls with turmeric paste. She collected betel-nut crackers, glass-bangles and embroidered shawls. When a miniature sewing machine—perfect, like a black kitten that purred softly when caressed—came home from the shop, Kalyani stitched at least a dozen doll jumpers with it.

A red-ribboned inheritance decreed that Ma would own

acres of land when she grew up. Nand Kumar, Ma's father, wore fur-collared overcoats tailored in London. He owned Lahore's first motorcycle and collected antiques that were kept in a large home with ripe fruits always on its trees and in its silver bowls. When Ma began to rescue hurt puppies for him to bathe and bandage and feed, he ordered for a doghouse.

Then little fires began to break out at night in distant neighbourhoods. And friends stopped dropping in for home-made jalebis and poetry during the evening mushairas in her home. The bearded shayars and clean-shaven poets no longer sat together to say 'wah wah' to each other. The invisible lines dividing the neighbourhood became charcoal dark and then red. Then one day Abdul, the old man who appeared at the doorstep every morning to chaperone Ma to school, stopped coming too.

Ma's father began to sleep with a revolver under his pillow. He told his wife that he was not going to leave the city; not being a Muslim did not mean that he no longer belonged.

Ma smelt fire one day while playing in her backyard and instinctively crept into the thin wooden womb of her new doghouse.

She did not yet know that her eleven-room home was being dismembered. She only heard lazy crackers. The kind people burst in Anarkali Bazaar during festivals. Only those crackers had never smelt like these. These smelt of leftover skin, burning walls and cold blood.

Even though she heard noises of celebration around a bonfire that could be seen by the whole of Lahore, she knew the joy was not hers to share. When it was all over,

Ma stumbled into the nearest home, not knowing that it belonged to a Muslim. She was bundled in a quilt, taken to a dark, quiet room and told not to answer if her name was called out aloud.

She slept through long days and sometimes could not sleep at all. Once or twice, a woman came into the room, held her tight and rocked her to sleep. Days and nights felt like worms slithering up and down her body and Ma lay under the cold quilt, hating the wet bed sheet and the food that first rose in her gut and then sputtered out from her bitter mouth like lava.

One night, she felt something caressing her and woke up to find the cold breath of a knife on her throat. A young male servant was leaning towards her slowly, but even before she could scream, he was slapped by a shadow and dragged away.

Next morning, she was told that she would be leaving for Kanpur, where her father's childhood friend had grown fresh roots years ago. No one else in India had tried to find her. Tai, a Hindu cleaning woman in the neighbourhood, took charge of Ma. Trains were no longer safe—sometimes the dead in them outnumbered the living. So Tai and Ma chose like many others to walk out of a history that was no longer theirs.

Fear flew above the walkers in frenzied circles, flapping its thick vulture wings. Men looked at the hungry bird gingerly and then looked away. The women chose not to look. They got busy with the babies wiggling in their arms and in their wombs. Spasms in souls and calves went unacknowledged. Everyone walked, clasping abridged life-stories in precious bundles.

Ma walked in gratitude because pain could be borne when it was not trapped alone in a doghouse. She memorised that human beings, even those with beribboned inheritances and revolvers under their pillows, were the most easily destructible things in the world. And if some doors and walls were safe and not being assaulted, it was only because the mob was destroying something else. She learnt that memories could be put in carts and whistled off with their bleeding roots to unfamiliar soils. And happiness was an open wound smarting under a sandpaper sky.

That she was not a person with two legs, two arms and a whole brain, but detachable from all sides at short notice. She was nothing but a nervous tic under the skin of a wounded giant inching painfully towards the future. A future that may not even exist. But Ma walked obediently till her deep-frozen pain rebelled. When it began to burn her, she was put on Tai's back. And then in strange, kind arms of people she did not know.

From these vantage points, she saw things even more clearly. She saw old men and women shiver outside the broken shells of lives they had taken for granted. She saw death. And the dead burning quietly in the peace of hasty pyres. At night sometimes, she crouched near a lonely funeral pyre, rubbing her cold hands, watching Tai stealthily cook daal khichdi in the flames. Ma saw that happiness could never be foretold, but pain could. When she slept at night, she knew that it was not obligated to break into a day.

4

THE SMELL MA had come to fear returned in waves
through the journey. The smell of cold flesh. It floated
above bushes and lonely carts abandoned by whatever had
been following them. Ma walked for weeks through the
tunnel of this smell. She ate and slept in it. When she woke
up, she felt like a hollow tree, emptied of life-giving, life-
feeling nerve ends, with grey dust swirling within.

Relief was a refugee camp in Amritsar. Here, Ma and Tai
boarded a train and many cities flickered past their window.
Nothing she saw told her that they had left an estranged
country and reached their own.

The journey was long, but not as long as the silence
between Ma and Tai. At the Kanpur station, they found a
rickshaw and reached Ma's final destination, a brown brick
house with a few gangly roses in its hard lap. Then Tai
spoke, 'Your parents chose to die before they could be
touched. Remember that when the pain gets too much.'

Soon, all the homes in Ma's neighbourhood erupted with
the Indian tricolour. Something somewhere had been set

free. But Ma's new home gave her nothing except an impersonal deference towards her grief. She watched the house from a distance. She saw a complete set of parents and two impervious little girls. When she could not bear to watch them, she saw chairs in intimate huddles, tables with tea-cup stains, middle-aged pillows with embroidered goodnights, flowerbeds being fed nutritious tea leaves and stolen scoops of dung. Photo frames with preserved childhoods.

Since not one thing out of so many was hers, she shrank from touching anything. She swam in the rooms like a troubled foetus in an unfriendly womb. She could not eat or breathe or sleep. She imagined the roof falling over her and the walls being scraped from the outside.

She chose not to remember the toy store, the sewing machine, her mother's shawls and her father silver oak chest. But memories spread like weeds in her veins and began to break into her dreams. She knew how to deal with nightmares, but the happy dreams ate into her. So after every happy dream, she sat next to a window in the second-floor guest room, trying to forget it.

One day, she saw a young man sitting by himself on the terrace opposite. He was so still that Ma noticed him only when he moved a hand to rub his jaw. Even though he was facing her window, he did not see her. Then suddenly he looked at her and smiled.

The next evening, Kanpur clutched its chest and its radio sets and wailed loudly and sobbed in long shudders over the news that Mahatma Gandhi had been killed by a mad man's bullet. The city's shock and anger passed Ma by and then decided to come back to remind her of her detachability.

The hair on the back of Ma's neck began to hurt when she heard, 'Throw that little refugee bitch outside. One of her kind must have shed Bapu's blood,' and she waited for the doors to crack, walls to give away and blood to be squirted on bed sheets, tables and chairs.

When the police descended on the house opposite hers, Ma learnt that the man she had seen the day before on the terrace had been Nathuram Godse. And that he had killed Gandhi. Because he wasn't a refugee and did not have a drop of partitioned blood, Ma was forgiven.

The tables and chairs began to look self-assured and safe and Ma took a hint from them and began to talk. First to Anamika and then to Manjari. Still, it was some time before the girls became Anna and Manna for her, and even longer before she could bring herself to play with them. She stayed away from the parents. From their kind, quiet father who smiled at her when he was not reading the newspaper. From the mother who smiled only when one of her own daughters came into the kitchen to eat the pakoras she fried every evening in a time-worn, black karahi.

Ma had been her father's princess and found it impossible to touch toys that had not been bought for her. She allowed herself a little affection for Anna's battered rabbit because it felt like her father's fur collars. When the girls threw it for the raddiwala who came to clean the house of newspapers and spent, old things, Ma could not sleep at night.

Watching her grieve, Anna scuffed and dirtied a new rabbit and gave it to her. But what she could not give Ma was the love that she commanded from the world by just being Anna. When the girls' Nanu paid them a visit, Ma became transparent and disappeared from everyone's vision.

Anna sometimes sought Ma out from the shadows and took her to the old man's room. She fished out biscuits from under his mattress and whispered, 'He likes to eat them alone but he shares them with us. Sometimes, he gives us cashew nuts and almonds too!'

But such moments of intimacy were rare, because Anna was her grandfather's favourite and was monopolised by him. Every morning, Ma saw him take his granddaughters out for a stroll. Once she followed them out of curiosity and saw the girls on a tea stall bench, their cheeks plump with sweetness and their hands plunging furiously into flaming jalebis.

She slunk away. And sometime later jumped from the second-floor window. But the result of that leap was not hers to choose, and so she decided that she only needed to live. The rest was preordained. After this shameful failure, she was sent away to a distant residential school in Firozpur because Anna's mother wanted her to be 'responsible for herself'.

The night before she was sent away, Ma could not sleep. She left her room to go to the terrace and just when she was about to climb the stairs, she heard footsteps behind her. She turned around and saw her father. He was dressed in a white kurta-pyjama. He was whole. Healthy. Safe. He told her, 'It's cold up there. Go back to bed.' So she did.

At Firozpur, Anna was the only one who wrote to her, and her letters grew longer with the years. Ma finished school and joined a women's college and worked for a degree with distinction from a hostel room. After her graduation, she did a teacher's training course because a letter told her, 'It will save us some bother if you knew how to fend for yourself.' Then she was posted to Panjhal as a primary school teacher.

She never learnt to be young, though a middle-aged teacher fell in love with her despite her grim coldness. He spied on her when she went into the jungle with a mug of water in the morning, and left his tired wife every night to stand outside Ma's window, begging her to let him in, just once.

Anna by then had been wooed and wedded by a tea-planting aristocrat from Ambrosa, a tea and pine valley in Kangra. She had met him on a holiday, married him within a month and borne him a son before their first wedding anniversary. Ma received a photograph of the two entwined together on their wedding day. Anna's eyes were crinkled as if they could not bear too much sunshine and her face was lifted to the sky even though she was only looking at her husband.

Manna had married above-average prosperity and was living in Mandi. Ma too was asked to come back because she was now ripe for marriage. She applied for leave and returned to Kanpur, fearing nothing except happiness.

5

HAPPINESS, MA HAD taught me, was a thorny, tricky animal. Wiggling in your arms. Threatening to wound you and get away.

But joy never hurt me as much as when I was in Ambrosa, around Samir, Anna aunty's son. Especially on the night of his tenth birthday, when Ambrosa's hills had turned into star heaps and Samir's long, linear, white-walled home glowed with delicious strawberry lights wrapped around its pillars. Inside the drawing room, they were loudly playing, *Chala jata hoon, kisi ki dhun mein, dhadhakte dil ke taraane liye.*

I looked at the wilfully dirty frock I had worn instead of the polka-dotted dress that Ma had broken two slit-backed, clay piggy banks for. My feet were bare and swinging half-heartedly from the porch bench where I sat like an urchin outside a bakery.

From here, I could see everything. Tall, gauzy orchids and wheat stalks nuzzling sprays of baby's breath in blue vases. Haughty Ikebanas preening from baskets. Little bottoms gliding from silk cushions and a baby centipede in the middle of the hall, swaying to music with scores of knocking, shining, happy knees.

Before the party, just before he went to his room to dress, Samir had asked me, 'What is wrong with you? You look like the ratty toy Dorky chews. You don't want to be at the party?'

I bit my lip and looked down, trying to say something, but by the time I looked up, he had grunted, shrugged and left.

Ma had tried to bring me inside and even threatened to never stitch another polka-dotted dress for me, and Anna aunty had cuddled me and asked me to 'reconsider' my 'shyness'. 'Why don't you want to come in? You know, the fun you can have now, you will never have on another day. This time will go and you will feel bad,' she had said, but I was glad that my knees and I were alone on the bench even though I could have been inside. I sniffed back my tears when Anna aunty, draped in a crisp, peach organdie saree, rolled out a cake train into the room with Cadbury's gems embedded on its ten rooftops. When the roar of Happy Burrday grew louder, I knew that Samir had expertly blown out twisted rainbow candles and sliced a chocolate cream bogey through and through.

I hungered for a little space next to Samir, for the caramel custard hillocks and stuffed bread triangles, for balloons which would soon release reckless streams of colour, for the sound of joy tinkling alongside ice cubes in tall glasses. But I did not leave the bench because I knew I would always be outside homes that glowed and buzzed like fireflies at dusk.

Life was easy for someone like Anna aunty. She was different from Ma and me. Even as a little girl, she had always got what she wished for. Sudden blossoms in secretive flowerbeds. A sunny day when she wanted to ride her bicycle in the front yard. Stars when she wanted to see them on a rainy night. Dresses to match all the seasons. And a husband who renamed his old, ancestral plantation home after her and pruned the flowerbeds around it to resemble the first letter of her name.

As a young girl, she once told Ma that one just had to tell life what one wanted. It always delivered. Ma did not believe her, and so, when Papu's name was circled in a newspaper matrimonial advertisement, she let go of her dream to be a civil servant and agreed to marry him.

Ma's wedding proved all her beliefs right. Everything went wrong. The ice cream melted too early. The Halwai, who had been celebrated for the feast served at Anna aunty's wedding, overcooked the pulav, browned the rabri and put too much salt in the matar-paneer.

The professional wedding mare supposed to bring Ma's groom to the wedding hall fell sick. Someone arranged for another mare at the last moment and did not disclose that, before her retirement, she had been used for police parades and once in a while to control riots. So when Papu grazed her hide accidentally, she took off, leaving the wedding dancers screaming incredulously.

The mare flew, taking the sehra and my raw-silk clad Papu on the ride of his life. Papu flung his sehra away from his face and grabbed the mare's neck with both his hands. He began to coo in honeyed Punjabi into its bristling ear, 'Uden jab jab zulfen teri O dulhan, kuwaron da dil machale'.

(He later roughly and inaccurately translated the words to Ma as 'When your mane flies, my bride, all young colts die of love'.) The mare liked that and began to preen and soon Papu and his dulhan were bounding and bonding around a play park in happy circles.

Papu had served the army in the Indo–China war, and his short service commission had prepared him for such an emergency. He knew how to tame recalcitrant mares who cared nothing for a groom's urgency to get to his bride. When he finally came to wed Ma, his was the only happy voice she heard through the muffled haze of her gota-spangled silk veil. He was singing a Sahir ghazal most appropriate for the occasion—*Tum ek baar mohabbat ka imtihaan toh lo*—willing Ma to test his love for her just once.

She came as a bride to Patiala in a bus pounding with Aasa Singh Mastana's folk songs with only a faint sense of disbelief. As she listened to *Kaali teri guth te paranda tera laal ni* (dark is your plait and red is your parandi), she knew that if Partition had not divided her life into two, she would still have been in Lahore. She would have been a frail, sheltered aristocratic beauty and not the daughter-in-law of a middle-class Punjabi family. Or the wife of a dream-smith without a livelihood. But she had been spat across a bloody border and so she trained her ears to politely clam up when her mother-in-law said, 'I don't like rifoojis. They spread misfortune wherever they go. You, my girl, need to thank your stars that you found someone like my son. He could have had anybody, but he chose you.'

The house was not very receptive either. Papu's forgotten ancestors had built it with a closed fist and it looked as if someone had asked it to shut up. It only looked inwards. None of its windows opened into unblocked skies. When it rained, its bare brick walls developed a grey snivel and the staircase between the terrace and the ground floor flooded. A small kitchen sat on haunches in one corner and accommodated only one person at a time. A hand-pump under the staircase was used to wash vessels, clothes and children. The women bathed in the kitchen.

Close to the kitchen were two Siamese rooms. The meshed window of one room looked at the hand pump. The room was called the 'drawing room', though no one was ever drawn to it. It had a jute charpoy, three chairs and a weepy bulb forced to burn till the family went to sleep. Vegetables were cut here. Tea was served to occasional guests. Unwashed nappies lay in piles. And feet unwillingly suspended themselves in air when Ma swabbed the grey, cement floor.

The other room opened into the street, its lone window gazing at someone's mossy wall where a peepal branch grew uproariously in a crack. Here, an anaemic cow with bad digestion was kept. Her odours seeped into everything. Even pillows and bath soaps.

The first floor had two bedrooms. None had doors and so gave away all their secrets to each other. One room belonged to Papu's elder brother, his wife and two children. Papu's mother slept in the other. Ma and Papu slept in the drawing room on a mattress that was rolled and put away in the morning. The house and the people in it gave Ma nothing.

But after a decisive night when she almost jumped from a bridge to her death with me in her womb, she decided to make peace with all of them. And to accept once and for all that her estrangement with joy was permanent.

Life became easier when she fell in love with Papu. With his broad forehead and his stubborn radiance. Together, they shut out the sour voices of the rest of the family and retreated into their own world. They began to joke about each other's feet. Hers were big. His were small and fine. He told her once, 'You are my morni, peahen. Lovely feathers. Who cares about the feet?' She laughed, 'And you are the sparrow. Lovely feet. Who cares about the rest of you?'

They laughed together about how he had tamed his wedding mare. He sang to her like an inspired poet. He read from his Kaifi Azmi booklet, 'Kee hai koi haseen khata har khata ke saath. Thoda sa pyar bhi mujhe de do, saza ke saath', (Each wrong that I did, though wrong was also beautiful so with every chastisement, love me a little too) and tried to make her understand that he would always make mistakes and she would have to forgive him because he loved her and her soggy, clammy heart. Her lone dimple. The clefts on her shoulders that he believed had carried wings in her previous birth.

He named her Rani, his queen. With this name, Papu reclaimed her back from her dead parents. Between her teaching job and his joblessness, whenever they met, they made the most of their shared lacks. I was eight months old inside her when Papu dared her to ride his scooter. She remembered her first miscarriage with a shudder, but took him on and celebrated her first shaky ride by going twice around the Shiva temple.

He cheered her on and bought her a faux fur coat with

her money from a pavement stall. Also a cone of spicy peanuts and lemon soda pop at Crystals where his college friend gave him endless credit. When her feet swelled up and she could not sleep through long nights, he told her about Sahir Ludhianvi. How he had fallen in love with Urdu poetry when he first saw this pock-marked, long-haired, dark-eyed, hypnotic poet at a mushaira.

He spoke as if there was nobody else in the room . . . he swept his hair back away from his face sometimes and kept his eyes closed. And he recited:

Aao ke koyi khwaab bunen kal ke vaaste . . .
Varnaa ye raat aaj ke sangeen daur ki . . .
Das legi jaan-o-dil ko aise ke jaan-o-dil . . .
Taa-umr phir na koyi haseen khwaab bun sake.

'Come, let us weave a dream together . . . or else this night of these hard times will poison the soul and the heart and render us incapable of dreaming ever again.'

Ma recited to him a nazm she had heard from a college friend, 'Garmiye hasratein nakaam se jal jaate hain . . . hum chiragon ki tarah shaam se jal jaatein hai.' I burn in the futile fire of my desire . . . I burn like a row of lamps whenever dusk falls. When she whispered the words to him, something swelled within her and threatened to burst because she remembered the dusk poets of Lahore and their sonorous voices.

She then told him about Lahore and let her tears wet his sleeve. He stroked her hair and said, 'My father taught me to recite the shlokas of the Bhagavad Gita when I was four. Then he taught me to read and write in Urdu. I was not born in Lahore like you and your father, my Rani, but I know what was taken away from you. When they burnt your home, they burnt generations of those who grew up like me, loving Krishna and Kaifi and the treasure of Urdu poetry . . . and the tehzeeb of loving that which is neither Hindu, nor Muslim, but belongs to both like the waters of Ganga and Jamuna.'

He also told her how he and the poet Basheer Badr had once recited their nazms at a mushaira in Patiala. 'And someone loved my nazm so much, he gave me a red, silk pouch full of silver coins!' he smiled. Not telling her that though he himself was happy enough to never try for another pouch, Badr went on to become a modern icon among post-Independence Indian poets.

Papu may have been blessed with inspiration, but he had never climbed any mountain for success. He had been happy just sitting at the bottom and singing to himself. And now he had his Rani to sing to. What more did he need? There were so many stories to share with her. He told her about the night when he was coming home after the late night show of the film *Ganga Jamuna*. Just that morning, Papu had become the president of the student's union in his college.

'Suddenly they surrounded me. A few jealous boys with seething hockey sticks. They were angry because I had beaten their favourite candidate by a few votes. But I knew then and I know now that men are not beasts. There is a moment just before they grow mad when even they know that. I grabbed that moment and began to talk about the film. It is so simple to cure all the evil in this world. Men kill because they forget momentarily what they love most in their lives. A man who loves something deeply cannot kill.

And if you talk to even a killer about his passion, he will put down his weapon and listen to you. People talk too much about what they hate. If they only talked about what they love. Before they could raise their sticks and their voices, I told them the whole story of the film, complete with dialogues. I told them how great Dilip Kumar was when he died. How even his eyes died with him . . .

'When I finished, there was nothing but silence and the boys were walking with me as if we had all known each other for years. They came with me till my door and then left.'

Another night, he told her about the day he and his Sikh friends screamed, 'Bole So Nihal . . .' and then brought down, with one shattering kick, the boundary wall of a neighbourhood rogue who made hooch in his backyard.

And then how a Hindi film actress had a crush on him in Kashmir when he was there on a budget holiday with college pals. How he could have been a steward aboard an international airliner or a tourism officer in Kashmir but chose to be free.

How he got a widowed cousin to marry again and protected her wedding ceremony from disapproving relatives. With hockey sticks and dozens of friends who were willing to use them if anyone dared to interrupt the ceremony.

How he had encouraged a young, suppressed girl in his mother's extended family to study, to speak aloud in declamation contests, to eat with forks and spoons and to dream big.

Ma began to see how much love Papu had and how little patience. She saw him rampaging across the house whenever his brother belittled him. And then remembered how many opportunities he had been given by fate to soar above No. 7, Bakshi Ganda Singh Street and how he had spurned each one because he just wanted to be where he was. Ma told herself that he was ocean trapped in a clay urn and one day would break free and change everything.

Papu broke free the night Ma cried out aloud in pain. She was giving birth to me in the 'drawing room' with the help of a mid-wife, and Papu winced every time she screamed. He scowled dangerously when Beeji, my grandmother said, 'Your woman looked bovine and lazy during her ninth month. I knew she would deliver a girl. A boy, even if he has one leg, has seed for the earth. What do I need a girl for?'

He shut his ears against the complaints of his brother's wife and sold the cow, and with that money bought a cot for the three of us and placed it where the cow used to suffer through her life. When Ma took me back to her job in Panjhal, he vowed that he would bring us back soon. He locked up his imagination, stopped writing imaginary editorials and began to check out classified facts in newspapers. Then the country went to war again. This time with its severed half across the border. The army beckoned veterans like Papu with juicy emergency commissions. He reapplied and was sent into the heart of battle. From an unnamed war front, he sent back a story that Ma re-read many times in the lantern light. Papu was driving a jeep with an officer friend through a ravine when bombs began to fall around them like parched autumn leaves. Papu was still singing *Main zindagi ka saath nibhata chala gaya* when his friend jumped out of the jeep and ran down a slope to hide in a deep, cool bunker. Papu stopped the jeep and took the key out of the ignition. He sat in his seat, waiting for the untimely shower to stop. He heard his friend screaming to be heard above the din, 'Veeren, you idiot. Get off that cow and get here.'

Papu turned his face to look at him and saw him raise an arm in a frantic signal before a bomb fell right on him and blew him into ribbons. The bombs stopped falling eventually and Papu sat alone in the jeep for a long, long time. He never sang that song ever again.

Then Papu got a family accommodation in Assam and asked Ma to leave everything and join him. He wanted to erase the poverty of their marriage. Ma was cold and lonely in Panjhal and was tired of hearing me call out to Papu in my sleep. So she fled towards bliss. So what if it was to shatter at some bewitched hour? She fled towards the uncluttered landscape of Missamari and to a flat with creamy walls. Towards kitchen cabinets with wire-mesh baskets for her spoons and ladles and wooden wardrobes bursting with new chiffons and Assamese silks.

Ma let her straight black hair open for the first time in her life. Her arms, with their missing angel wings, and her large, almost transparent brown eyes began to stop conversations. She dressed mostly in diaphanous blues. Her eyebrows turned into high-winged birds in glorious flight. Her high forehead lost its worries and her skin could not contain the joy in her veins when Papu's smooth, deep voice floated out of loud-speakers during equestrian shows.

She learnt not to smile too much when he recited Urdu poetry at amber parties redolent with kabab juices. She learnt not to be startled by the opulent, stuffed python strung across the entrance of the Officers' Mess. And learnt to walk bravely into rosy, perfumed spaces. And to appreciate the genteel politics of warbling laughter and the futile beauty of pink-tipped hands. And the useless pleasures of riverside picnics and vinegar dipped onion bulbs on toothpicks.

She happily sent a large amount of money to Papu's family and even a long, angry letter from Patiala accusing her for distancing him from his 'near and dear ones' did not spoil her happiness. But life continued to remind her that she was not to make the mistake of being too happy. And so, one day, a three-tonne army lorry carrying a group of Sunday revellers inexplicably fell into a ditch. The only one injured in the accident was Ma. She had a dislocated shoulder and a bruised knee.

Ma defied her health and got pregnant. She had lost one son and she wanted another. 'I don't want you to be alone,' she told me. She ate pineapples and fish and rested in her bedroom with a magazine. One morning, I snuggled up to her and began to cry. She held me close and then I told her, 'Ma, I saw Anurag, my brother. He was sitting on a very high wall. He could have just sat there. But he jumped.'

She sprang up in pain and looked at me with fear. In the evening, she was taken to the hospital. A few days later, she came home. Alone. And began to feast on Missamari with a vengeance. She baked cakes, fed hungry orderlies and played in her life-sized doll house without any fear of a hungry mob outside her gate.

Even my attempts to disrupt her fleeting harmony did not rattle her. But one day, when his short-service commission ended, the make-believe perfection was left behind as Papu gathered Ma, me and his songs and headed back to Patiala.

Ma repeated a lesson she had taught herself as a little girl. It did not matter one way or the other. Life never asked for one's opinions. It did not recognise a woman's desperate love for a house with sun-lit, flower-filled balconies. It would mercilessly go in a direction it had preconceived for itself.

So she sat in a train with acceptance and the few belongings she had brought from Missamari, and let herself remember another departure from happiness, many years ago. She was thankful that, this time at least, she was not travelling with strangers.

6

UNLIKE MA AND Papu, I had no memories of Patiala or its greasy hardware shops. At six, I had no recollection of the grey belches of its bus station or clusters of migrant labourers who sat on their haunches at Quila Chowk with paint brushes and carpentry tools, waiting for the small jobs that genial Sikh contractors would give them.

Papu's brother, my uncle Naren, had moved with his family to Delhi much before our arrival and we eased with grateful relief into the butter warmth of a house that was the cusp between the Hindu homes of Bakshi Ganda Singh Street and the Sikh pride of Jattanwala Chauntra. We were always the first to hear Ek Onkar Satnam, that Sikh devotees sang in whispers on shivering morning streets to usher in Nanak's birth.

We woke to Patiala's morning breath fragrant with shabads from a loud-speaking Sikh gurudwara. Filmy bhajans trickled out from a Durga temple in Sirhindi Bazaar and a lone azaan emanated from a mosque in Adalat Bazaar. Patiala embraced everyone who walked in, with its undemanding squalor. It made you hurt for its fading landmarks. And its fading memory. Few people except Papu remembered that magnificent kings had ruled Patiala till Yadvendra Singh became the first Indian prince to sign the Instrument of Accession and integrated Patiala, with all its bejewelled royal bravado, seamlessly into independent India. Papu had been a child when Patiala had lost its royal privileges but it pained him to see how the dying arches and disintegrating gates stood alone, breathing their last above expanding bazaars. Ma wondered sometimes if the tall gates in her Lahore had died too.

Every night, Papu, Ma and I walked to the temple in Quila Chowk, bought milk barfi and flowers and climbed its mud-stained, wet marble steps to pray to a blue Shiva.

We walked through Acharon Wala Bazaar, where olives, slivers of mangoes and lemons glowed like gems in glass jars and floated in mysterious juices. We tasted them from little spoons that fastidious shopkeepers extended. We never sniffed at the pickles because greedy nostrils could impair their flavour forever. We occasionally gave in to the late evening Punjabi cravings for fruit chaat, thick, white, cream kulfis and dark gulab-jamuns fuming on roadside carts.

We enjoyed the drama of floor-to-ceiling stacks of embroidered jootis and the sight of salesmen climbing ladders to get to them. The jootis, in high heels, pointed toes and all sizes were the pride of Patiala's women. As were the tasseled parandis they wore in their long braided hair and the caressing silk drawstrings that they slipped in the waistbands of their salwars. For them were also Adalat Bazaar's meadows of colourful Phulkari dupattas. The embroidered Phulkari stars were like the Punjabi spirit.

Woven with different skeins into a tight fabric that nothing could tear apart.

Every Sunday, we had aloo tikkis and casatta ice cream at Kashyap's, a small, narrow eatery in Adalat Bazaar and then walked off the calories in the Baradari Garden. We sat on green, iron benches, pressing bare heels in red earth, counting the twelve gates opening into the garden, counting the countless trees and trying not to notice couples on secretive first dates. Once when we passed by a couple with daringly fused hands, Papu looked the other way and began to tell me loudly about how the legendary cricketer Lala Amarnath used to give cricket lessons to both his sons in this 'very same garden'.

He also walked me occasionally to Quila Mubarak, one of the last few brick-and-mortar memories of a lost kingdom. Whenever we saw the fort, Papu described to me the ferocious passion of a Baba Ala Singh who had built it. The fort was still the heart of Patiala, even though it beat only faintly now. Its lifeblood was visibly oozing out and the walls were coming apart stealthily, even as they tried to accommodate two Victorian statues, bird-droppings, a museum packed with royal vintage cars, whale-sized cut-glass chandeliers, shining shields and armoury, along with scruffy government offices.

Visiting the Moti Bagh Palace was a ceremonial ritual. We went there once every month because Ma loved walking through its grounds designed just like the Shalimar Gardens of Lahore. I loved the Sheesh Mahal and its walls aglow with Kangra and Rajasthani paintings, the rich, old patinas of colours from all seasons and the way all of Patiala's rulers glowered at me intensely from their sumptuous portraits in the museum hall.

Then we walked back to our home, past Dev Taya's curd and mithai shop. Or sometimes, through a short-cut reeking of a rancid coal shop, the cloying, greasy sweetness of a small dairy and the rumbling warmth of a flour mill. I loved Bakshi Ganda Singh Street's musty womb. It gave me immense relief. I flourished in its dark entrails, among its mouldy, biscuit walls.

There was so much to do here. Run around with scruffy children playing I Spy. 'Icebice' for them. Put Ma's only lipstick in a wall cavity of our house and pretend to be Mamaji, the Sikh grocer who sold pigeon-holed merchandise and cheap cosmetics from his tiny shop in Jattan Walla Chauntra. Or steal a piece of coal from a clay angeethi that burnt through the winters in my grandmother Beeji's room. And then draw Dalda ghee tins complete with their curling palm trees on neighbouring walls. I wasn't a smudge in Patiala. I blended in.

I learnt new names, memorised new neighbours.

There was the cat-eyed Prakasho running a steel vessel manufacturing unit in her backyard with her husband. They played cards on the terrace and never went anywhere without each other.

There was Ashok, a bachelor, who emerged from his house only to throw strange vials and spent syringes outside his door. When he walked, it was as if he had been jabbed in the thigh with a knife.

Parveen di, who worked in a bank and had a TV and a phone connection. Naveen, the motor mechanic. His wife Shano, who had fallen in lust with her young tenant. Sheela Panditani, the Hindu priestess who did not know the scriptures but made up for it by being poor. She survived because she was given alms at every happy occasion and was fed on death anniversaries. There was Shuki, the diabetes-ridden bitter-half of Som Halwai, perpetually boasting about their sweet shop in Adalat Bazaar.

Then there was Mitthu, an old crab living alone in a big, imposing house. Clawing at children playing outside his front door. And being stoned by them occasionally. Swarna, a young typist living in a Sikh household as a paying guest.

And Bebe, an old woman who lived noiselessly in the house next to ours.

There was, however, a lot of noise around us. Neighbours shouted over common walls to each other and then made up loudly. Ma quickly became the universal favourite by virtue of her quiet tongue.

Two white-bearded Sikh brothers smiled broadly whenever she went to their vegetable shop next to the big banyan tree in Sarhindi Bazaar. They called her Beebaji with affection and told her, 'Whenever you come, the shop attracts customers. Just like a slab of sweet gur invites flies. Here, take some oranges for the little girl. No, don't pay for them.'

Life flowed easily. Every day I stepped over the jutting stones in the unpaved street and the fading memories of Missamari to help Ma get the family quota of municipality water from the public tap. I let Ma walk home with a brimming bucket and stood next to the tap to guard two virgin buckets from thirsty cows.

Patiala gushed, flowed and swirled around us, filling our parched hearts much like the water that flowed from the spoutless public tap and was lapped up by our buckets. We celebrated everything: the births of Sikh Gurus, victories of

Hindu Gods over evil, the arrivals and departure of seasons. Patiala's bazaars chattered like overfed, happy children and grew fatter with rainbow sweets, lights and firecrackers during the weeks leading up to Guru Nanak's birthday and Diwali.

We feasted for Vaman, a particularly interesting avatar of Vishnu. And on Vaman Dwadshi, we happily clogged the bazaars with hundreds of others to cheer a carnival of Gods on floats. The Gods wore wigs, blue makeup and gold-painted paper halos. They all sat on cardboard lotuses or swans. Shiva sat cross-legged, plastic snakes around his neck against a backdrop of cotton-patched Himalayas. Ram and Laxman struck militant poses and aimed at an invisible Ravana with their silver bows. An orange-hued Hanuman tried to fly with the help of metal wires. Divine halos squirmed in uneasy circles.

A running trophy with peeling copper was won by the most imaginative float. Another running trophy was given to the best team of tipri dancers who practised the whole year in their neighbourhood for this one moment of transcendence. The whole town swayed with them when they danced with slim tipri sticks in their hands, slowly at first and then in impossible multiplications of feet, arms and heads.

No one knew or cared whether Lohri was a Sikh or a Hindu festival. Everyone threw jaggery sweets and waste paper into clumsy bonfires to welcome spring. The children from both sides got mixed up and went from house to house with their lanterns. They sang *Sunder Mundariye* before indulgent grandmothers and got their share of sweets and pennies. I watched adoringly, as blue-skirted Nihangs rode their horses in processions and sparred with shining swords. I went with Papu and Ma to Dukh Niwaran, the gurudwara where multi-religious grievances were healed by the resident spirits of Sikh Gurus.

On Hoi Ashtami, my Beeji made a goddess out of cowdung, clay limbs, mirrors and tissue paper and stuck her on the wall. Then we prayed to Her. During Dussehra, Papu took me and other neighbourhood children to the large parade ground near Mall Road. There we watched a firecracker-stuffed, twenty-feet-tall Ravana fall to his doom.

Then we walked back to a home that belonged to us. Irrevocably. With all its flaws, its cracks, its rainy windows, its damp darkness. Beeji was now too old to lament the lack of a grandson or to resent the dry, infertile womb of her daughter-in-law. Papu had begun to write for a local newspaper. We all lived an unthreatened existence. We were happy.

7

'IT IS WRITTEN that Patiala will be swallowed by its river,' Beeji told me one day when it began to rain, and didn't stop. 'When I was young, whenever it rained like this and the river got angry like a jealous wife, the raja offered it jewels, sought its forgiveness, and only then would it calm down.'

She watched the skies in fear and worried for the shuddering house next door, which had no cement—it was made of just raw courage and mud and the memories of Bebe. She was Beeji's only living friend. Bebe was not a small piece of fluffy white cotton candy like Beeji. She was an oak, now bent and old but still hard to ignore. No one could pass her by without a reverential nod. But for all her stern stillness, the water in her kiln-baked pot was still the sweetest and the coolest. The rotis that puffed up on her mud-and-iron stove were the softest. Before the monsoon rattled and shook it, her house had walls of pure peace. She had no electricity and at night, only a kerosene flicker lit up one window.

Bebe was deep brown and smooth like her home, and the two were inseparable. If Papu and Beeji had not told me, I would not have believed that Bebe had once been a broad-shouldered, trusted spy in the raja's army. Or that she had often disguised herself as a man to hunt down his foes. I overheard Beeji telling Ma once, 'When Gagandeep was ripe for love and passion, she wore loose, long clothes to hide her breasts from suspicious eyes and a Sikh turban to conceal her long hair. When it was dark, she and her horse became one and streaked quietly through the night. She still has a gun rusting in one of her many tin boxes.'

On retirement, she received a square of land from the raja. By then she was too spent to build too much, and so decided to settle for a hollow mud shell. But the house had seen too many cruel seasons and was not aging as well as her. On the third afternoon of ceaseless rain, it was desperately trying to hold onto the ground with shivering claws. It looked as if one of Bebe's old enemies had returned from the dead to chip at her gleefully.

When the windowpanes in our house grew louder than our voices, Papu jumped from the diwan in the drawing room and ran towards the terrace. I followed him, squelching the stairs behind him. He leaned across the parapet and began to shout, 'Bebe? Bebe . . . e . . . e?'

Bebe appeared in a small, round, iron-barred window. She growled, 'What is it Veeren? Why are you shouting my house down?'

Papu and I stuck together. Like swathes of wet tissue-paper. Papu shouted back, 'You need to get out Bebe. I am coming to get you.'

'I am not leaving this place, Veeren. I will die with it. I have nowhere to go.'

'Go to your village. Stay with your brother. That is your home too.'

'I have always lived alone and I am too old to change,' she hollered back. 'And,' she added, 'my raja gave me this place. I can't leave it and go.'

'The raja is gone, Bebe. And this house will go too. I am coming to get you,' Papu said and ran down the stairs. I went behind him but he stopped me at the door. 'You stay here. The house may fall the moment I step in,' he told me and disappeared.

Two minutes later, they appeared. I couldn't see her face in the rain but I knew that Bebe was crying. Papu held her with one arm and carried a tin box in another. I wondered if her gun was in it.

They were a few steps away from me when the mud shell exploded behind them. There was a roar and both Papu and Bebe turned to watch. The roof was first to go. When the roar stopped, there was nothing left to look at. The next morning, Papu took Bebe to Sanaur.

Sometimes Beeji and I went in a cheerful bus to visit her. We hurtled past ripe gold fields, brick-red farmhouses and long minutes of nothingness. Bebe lived among green and golden ber trees, pots of frothy buttermilk, surrounded by mustard, husk and cow dung smells and sugarcane fields. She wasn't happy but was reconciled to change. She was treated well by her brother and his children.

She told Beeji, 'Things are changing. The children don't want to tend the fields anymore. They want to get rich. Fly to other countries. We can't stop them but what will happen to our farms and to us if the children leave?'

Then one gnarled hand reached out for another. Beeji's

cataract-filmed eyes grew greyer and Bebe's deep wrinkles filled up with pain. Then Bebe gave me a one rupee coin to buy a cream kulfi. I came back home, my stomach full of bers, buttermilk and a little rust from the one-eyed kulfi-vendor's old ice-box.

Bebe died a few months later and Beeji sneaked away too, to join her within a year. And for many months after she was gone, I continued to hear Beeji's wide-awake wooden slippers on the stairs at exactly five-thirty in the morning, the muffled chanting of her favourite shloka and her morning conversation with herself. And one night when I was gathering Ma's bedsheets from the clothesline on the terrace, I saw Beeji and Bebe. They had a lantern and were looking for something they had left behind in the house that was no more. I tried to call out to them but they melted into the night like two ravens.

8

BAKSHI GANDA SINGH Street was infested with television antennae now, and there was one on almost every roof. We did not have one yet on ours, so we made do with Papu's transistor and Ma's radio.

On the night of a World Cup hockey final between India and Pakistan, we decided to sleep on the terrace. To watch the stars while Papu listened to the commentary. He had been a hockey player in college and loved the game with all the unspent passion of the goals he had not struck. His favourite player was Ashok Kumar, legendary Olympian Dhyan Chand's son. 'He is his father's son. If anyone can win this match, it is my Ashok,' Papu told us. Ma and I moved on our cot in anticipation as the transistor sputtered and the commentator tried desperately to be heard above the high-strung spectators but Papu cut him short. He already knew the course of the match. 'Ashok's going to do it. He moves like a breeze on the ocean. The moment he gets a ball, the Pakistanis will part like water.'

Ma smiled in the night. Then Papu understood, 'You are

amazed that it matters so much to us to win against each other? We were one country, right? Rani, if we sweep aside all memories and all the pain we have given each other, we will get past the need to win at all costs. If we can't forget, then it is better to score goals than to fire bullets. Remember, I fought the Pakistanis. It was not pleasant. At least, on a playground, everyone lives.'

Then Ashok Kumar scored a goal and Papu yelled. He jumped from his bed and I from mine and we both danced along with hundreds of Indians oceans away who had watched Pakistani waters part for a little Indian with a sparring hockey stick.

In the morning, I went still smiling to my school in a rickshaw pulled by Ram Pyare, a Bihari migrant, and settled in my niche on the extra wooden seat he had fixed to accommodate more legs than the rickshaw was meant to carry.

The school I had been going to for a few years had once been a royal retreat with long motorcades crawling out of its porch. No liveried English band played now in the high-ceilinged, wood-panelled ballroom; instead Mr Tuli, our little, squeaky-voiced librarian, presided over shining reading tables, hollow whispers and steel cupboards filled with books.

The library was the school's core and many large classrooms surrounded it. Their window grills were lacy, their pillars white, their skylights stained with rainbows. The beauty was, however, not uniform. Many awkward rooms had been built haphazardly to accommodate more students.

The rooms were redeemed by the old trees growing

around them in disciplined rows. The most dramatic was the lipstick tree, with buds you could peel to reveal miraculous, orange-coloured lipsticks. There was the lone pine with its fragrant scabby bark and cones. A banyan. Many mango trees. Lemon-scented bushes bordering neat pathways. The jamun tree was the discordant note though, in this perfection. It grew purple with luscious jamuns in summer, but spoilt it all because it stood next to a toilet. The jamuns fell right into the purple island in front of the toilet door and got squashed under hurrying little shoes. Their sour-sweet smell mixed up unforgivably with the pungency of urine.

My school and its grounds reminded me of Missamari, its neat rows that never frayed around the edges, its monsoon-washed trees and its clear-cut sunsets. Sometimes I woke up from dreams where an oozing community tap in a jungle of green-mossed, grey and brown homes melded into a stream in a pine forest. I suddenly became conscious of the burnt porridge smell of my street and walked through it, holding my breath.

Sometimes, I sat alone on my terrace to watch kites of the deepest pinks, blues and greens and pet pigeons being guided back home with flailing arms, strange, guttural, human-pigeon noises. I wished I could fly too. Somewhere. With someone. To someone.

A few months after the hockey match, as the rickshaw rumbled towards the school under Ram Pyare's dark, sinewy legs, Mohan, my seat-mate whispered, 'You all know something? We are all under Emergency. You know what that means? I know—my Daddy told me. It means every wall, every rickshaw, even this one, every place has a tape-recorder fitted to it. So anyone who talks loudly will be caught on tape and then sent to jail. And who knows what will happen there? Your kidneys may be taken out. Your legs may be broken.'

So for the next few days, we all guarded our kidneys and whispered watchfully. We only began to talk normally when Ram Pyare assured us that his rickshaw had been debugged of all sorts of incriminating tape-recorders.

Sometime later, I met Samir.

I was eight, the summer holidays were on and Ma sold a gold bangle, told Papu that she needed see her Anna and took me to Ambrosa. We had met, I was told, in Kanpur when I was very small, but I did not remember him at all. I only remembered that, in Missamari, his voice had once travelled into my world over a surprisingly clear telephone line. He had said, 'I have oranges. Come and eat them,' and it had warmed my bones with pride. It was a strong voice, echoing of a well-rooted, large, limitless life.

The family lore went that Samir was born ten days before his due date. It was early morning and Inder uncle, Anna aunty's husband, had gone to attend to an emergency at his plantation office. Anna aunty was in bed, drinking ginger tea. Even before she could finish her tea, her son tore his way out. When a housemaid rushed in, hearing Anna aunty's cries, he was impatiently trying to end things even before they had begun. Her gentle hands clasped him and eased him out from a bloody river. When he took his first breath in her wet hands, a window rattled and the curtains billowed with the mountain breeze. That is when Anna aunty decided to call him Samir.

And because Anna aunty always shared all her gifts with Ma, I too was given a part of Samir's name.

Ma and I slept through the night journey to Ambrosa on a single train berth.

We had never been to Kanpur after coming back from Missamari because she still remembered our last visit there. The terse smiles round the dining table, sentences dying mid-air when she entered a room, the walls that clammed up at her touch and mine.

She knew Ambrosa would be different. We ate bananas and drank malted milk from a thermos, one of Ma's surviving wedding gifts. When the sky turned a pale pink rose, our train reached the Asankot railway station. There, the toy train to Ambrosa was steaming with impatience. Its baby coupes had no berths. Just hard, blue-painted, bus-stop benches. We chose one and sat down to peel ourselves some oranges. There were others around us but Ma and I never noticed people. We never spoke to strangers. We never smiled at them. Ma's investments in people were selective and soul-deep. I had taken after her though I didn't know it then.

After the orange peels were stuffed in a paper bag and put away, I looked out of the window. The earth had melted into a cloud and the train was now just a thread running through it. Whenever mist thinned, I saw stone pathways and little homes with dark mouths and silver hair. Old men bunched up in sunny patches. Domesticated trees watching over cows, goats, hens. Marigolds blooming in tin canisters and then giving away to larger, bigger things like waves of paddy. And sudden bridges with white water frothing under their arches.

Sometimes, I could see nothing but furiously speeding trees with blurred monkeys. The mountains were dark green and their long, brown cracks were filled with thin, curly spools of water. The clouds had risen above the earth completely by now, to reveal with a flourish, the raging green fire of pine groves. A fire that had a translucent core, a fuzzy halo of sunlight and emerald breath.

Ambrosa's railway station was a wet painting with mountains on one side, mist on another and railway tracks in between. I saw no greys. Not even on the platform. Its silver was untarnished by footsteps. As if no one before me had ever stepped on it. We climbed a flight of wide stone steps edged with flowering cement pots. Walked through a peach brick station building, topped with a green, corrugated roof and supported by faded wooden pillars. The station was unperturbed, as if it had never heard the rumble of a train. We left behind the waiting taxis, bantering coolies and all human voices. Ma carried our suitcase and we both walked out of the station. Letting the cool, tingling breath of the hills pare off musty layers of stale sorrow from our skin.

The road thinned and then trickled through thick parallel columns of pine trees. Sunlight escaped from the masterful and dense, strong-knuckled and forbidding pines and fell near our feet in droplets. After their intense silence came the bazaars. Brimming with rich tourists and the things they could buy. And middle-class travellers on wistful budgets eating puffed rice, softies and bhel puri in paper cones.

Multicoloured sweaters trotted on ponies past restaurants. Honeymooning couples huddled on stone benches. Brides clinking blood-red bangles. Grooms with new cameras dangling around their necks. Buddhist prayer flags.

Hanuman and Durga shrines carved into mountain sides.

Ma stopped next to a food shack called Lovely Dhaba and we both laughed at the signboard flapping bravely in the wind. She ordered hot milk and jalebis for me. 'I don't want to you to be too hungry when you reach Anna's house,' she said, following every piece that travelled from the chipped plate into my mouth. Then the bazaars were swept aside by paddy fur, quilted tea-gardens and hills polka-dotted with sheep. Chawli, Ambrosa's little river, sanguine and lazy like the long notes of a tourist's mouth-organ, appeared. Running like a little girl through the valley, jumping over shiny beds of smooth stones, tumbling down from the arms of Harigiri, Ambrosa's patriarch mountain range wrapped up in a misty shawl.

The tea gardens were no longer distant rectangles but tactile slopes and the road twisting through them was like living satin. Looping and curling with a purpose that Ma and I could not yet fathom. Ma smiled, 'This is Anna's Perfect Eight. That's what she calls this road. It really does make an eight. A perfect one. With two perfect halves running into each other.'

A few women picking tea leaves directed us to Annaville's big metal gate. A guard waved us in and the gate swung open with insolent creaks. We began to climb down a flower-fringed slope. Then Annaville appeared. White shoulders weighed down by a shawl of pink bougainvillea. And my life fell off my bones and was left behind.

9

ANNAVILLE WAS A long, red-roofed secret that must have throbbed in a dreamer's heart, more than a century ago. Now she stretched from hope to fulfilment in a graceful sprawl. Breathing softly under ivy, smelling the blossoms at her feet and the orange buds around her many white arms.

Her breeze-cooled veranda watched Ma and me with unblinking windows. Then she turned away and began to survey a large green velvet square with a lily pond, mottled bird baths with crumbling leaves, an old, old Buddha bathing forever under a lacy waterfall, and 'A'-shaped rose beds that its present master had created for his wife.

We walked on brown, green, mossy shadows of silver oaks, past stone benches and a bougainvillea canopy to a perfectly whitewashed and uninterrupted Ever After.

Towards a veranda daring us to disrupt the poise of a wine-red floor and the harmonious silence of white painted, bamboo settees. A secret room, deep in the house, played some music and I turned just in time to see the garden rising and falling to keep up with it.

Then I saw Anna aunty glimmering on the veranda floor. My eyes slowly rose to her powder blue bell-bottoms, her beaded lace top, her lustrous bob and the two turquoise stones in her ears. Her bare arms were cast in bronze, her mouth was a ripe lotus and her eyes grew dark and light at will when she smiled.

I understood why Ma believed that the world could not deny her Anna anything. She kept it beautiful just by being in it. I held my breath when she bent down and imprinted me with her bone-deep fragrance and with a little of that joy only she knew how to find and to keep forever.

'And this is Samir,' she pointed towards a camel-coloured suede jacket and a pair of brown corduroys. The boy inside them was hard to look at. Perhaps because of the sunlight that flowed like honey through his skin. Or because my shoulders had swallowed my neck and my head. Or because of the ease with which he stood with his hands in his pockets. When Samir walked us into the drawing room, my legs froze at the threshold and did not move even when he turned back and looked at me. I noticed that he smiled with his mouth closed.

Anna aunty leaned against a marble-chested, spindly-legged console and caressed a bunch of long-stemmed yellow rose buds. She and Ma were laughing. I had never seen Ma laughing with her head on her knees and her arms holding her stomach. Samir and I had been forgotten.

'And you slept through it all,' Anna aunty gurgled through a story about a monkey mother who had slipped her baby through the window grill in Kanpur to taste five bowls of kheer arrayed on the dining table when the family was away for an after-dinner, pre-dessert walk. Everyone except Ma. And Ma had fallen asleep in a chair waiting for them. Even the monkey child had not bothered to acknowledge her and had proceeded to dip his fingers in every bowl.

I did not find the story funny at all. I walked away to settle in a window-seat, trying not to disturb the satin cushions. The sun had vanished behind the mountains and the valleys were all red and the tea gardens black. Samir was throwing ginger cookies at a panting little dog. 'His name is Dorky. He is a Lhasa Apso,' Samir said, without looking at me. Many cookies later, when Dorky caught one, Samir patted him and smiled at me. I tried to smile back but only managed a scowl.

Then an old man, older than Anna aunty's acquaintance with Annaville, slowly walked in to unload before us a dark chocolate cake stuffed with walnuts and a jug twinkling with pineapple juice. There was already so much on the table. I had always wished to taste the red, glinting twin cherries on cherry blossom shoe-polish tins and now they had magically multiplied and fallen into a heap in a blue-and-white bowl. Next to them were thick white pastries bursting with pineapple squares. I did not like it when Samir took one pastry right from the middle and hollowed out the pretty picture.

All the lamps in the room had been lit except for the pink tulip chandelier at the centre. Samir saw me looking at it and said, 'We light this one only when we have parties. Ma will light it on my birthday. Soon.' A jeep growled in the driveway and Anna aunty flew to the door. When Inder uncle walked in, I noticed that he also smiled with his mouth closed.

Annaville had more corridors than Bakshi Ganda Singh Street had lanes and we walked through the longest one with Anna aunty after dinner. To a room just across Samir's. Ma and I lay awake for a long time, looking at the wood-panelled, sloping ceiling, the layered curtains, a study desk with fresh stationary and sharpened pencils. We both had bed-side tables and a stained glass lamp each. And rugs on both sides of our large bed.

I did not leave the bathroom in the morning till Ma discreetly knocked on the door and said, 'It is alright. The tub will still be there tomorrow.' I reluctantly left the bathroom and the little flowering pots on its window ledges, the towels stacked in a pinewood cupboard and the crystal bottles that could make the bathtub bubble with just a swish.

The days at Annaville bubbled away like a clear stream, gently washing over me. The frightened little animal crouching under my skin began to breathe in tandem with Annaville's becalming heartbeat. Every afternoon, when the house dozed, I walked barefoot on the badminton court to warm my soles, to smell the fruit orchard and to climb up the rope ladder of Samir's tree house where walls of dried leaves, bamboos and cane mats harboured toy guns, slings, a bow and an arrow.

I discovered all the hushed pathways around Annaville. I learnt when the silver oaks sighed the most. I did not yet know the names of all the flowers but I knew how many of them slumbered at dusk. My nose knew the salty sweetness of marigolds. The wet velvet fragrance of red roses. I learnt how to lift dewdrops from broad, glossy leaves. How to make a daisy, pebble, leaf, grass perfume.

One afternoon, Samir joined me in the garden. Looking gold-buffed in a red pullover. With the powder-puffed Dorky biting the hems of his jeans. Samir shooed him away and said, 'When I was very small, I used to dig the buttercups with a spoon!' I watched him. The sun fading around his edges. I realised my mouth was open. I closed it. Suddenly he laughed.

'What?' I asked him.

'Nothing,' he said.

That evening he took me, Dorky and a few friends to the garden for a picnic. We walked to the waterfall tumbling over Anna aunty's beloved Buddha. Under its shivering sheet of glass, was a squirming swarm of tadpoles. We took off our shoes to let the cold water scald our feet. When I began to shiver, Samir took off his jacket and wrapped its sleeves around my neck. He said, 'You are so small. Girls are small. But they are prettier than boys.' We ate from little china plates that Anna aunty had packed in a wicker basket. After I had licked the last trace of sauce from it, Samir washed my plate in the stream and scowled at a boy who was trying to scrape a tiny mole off my neck with his yellow nail. 'She is very small. Don't trouble her,' he said in a cold, ketchup-flavoured voice.

From then on, he took it upon himself to show me something new each day. He took me to the cow shed and patted its inmates on their wet bread noses, 'This thin one is Saudamini. This one with the fat cheeks is Vasundhara. This yellow one is Kanak . . .'

Samir told me all about Annaville's maids. All seven of them. 'The thin one is Suman. See how she dusts all the lamps and the pictures? Sometimes she gets bored. Then she goes and chats up Tek Singh. The driver. I think they will get married. But then he already has a wife. That is her elder sister Brinda. She brushes all the carpets and loves them like they were her pet dogs or something! And she keeps an eye on Suman *all the time*! She always follows Suman to the garage and scolds both Tek Singh and her. That is Satya. That is Meena and that is Shanti. They mop all the floors and it is better not to speak to them when they are at it. They are very cranky in the morning. Mohini and Seema dust and wipe the furniture. They are very slow. Sometimes they take half a day to finish one couch.'

He threw his room open for me and let me rummage through the piles of comics in his room. And hardbound volumes of Amar Chitra Katha crammed with Vedic warriors, jealous Gods, lovely princesses and miracles. He drew a hopscotch square on the terrace for me. Sometimes, he put a stool near his hammock for me to climb into the cushion nest easily. He let me play with his planes, his crayons and occasionally let me use his study-table to draw.

I rarely saw Inder uncle but sometimes he singled me out for sunshine on a cold day and brought me little gifts of colouring pens and chocolate boxes. He was a little like the misty Harigiri. Fair, square-jawed and averse to stooping. No one had ever seen him break the perfect symmetry of his body with sloppiness. He was always taut. And no one could ruffle his hair or box him playfully over the dinner table except Anna aunty.

Every evening Anna aunty changed into a fresh dress, put a rose in her hair and sat down with a pot of lemon tea in the veranda to wait for him. No one disturbed them till all the tea in the pot was spent. Then she put on a large apron with quilted strawberries and gave finishing touches to the dinner. The table was set around eight. After the last plate was taken away, Anna aunty and Inder uncle left together for their room.

It was the prettiest room in Annaville. With a wine-red armoire, a lacy cloud above the white bed and fresh flowers on its tables and in the window boxes. Sometimes she opened her drawers to let me play with her jewellery. She had emerald peacocks for her ears, little ruby birds and pearl daisies for her neck, little diamond moons for her wrists and gold nets that covered her shoulders.

'One day, it will all go to Samir's bride,' she would say. She turned over her dressing table to me and let me choose from hair-clips covered with painted apples, genteel shampoos, bags of dried orange peels and nail-polishes. I caressed the dresses in the armoire and touched silver and golden-hearted buttons, diamond-fired collars. I glided my fingers over zari borders, silk pipings, embroidered yokes and long panels of mist.

Anna aunty and Ma spent a lot of time talking. The only time Anna aunty was not with Ma was when Inder uncle was in the house. Only Anna aunty knew how to make cheese sandwiches the way he liked it, so no one entered the kitchen while she sliced large chunks of home-made bread. Inder uncle sat in a breakfast niche next to her. Looking at the tendril of hair fluttering under her ear and at the bronze shoulder blades heaving above the bread.

When he left, I filled in for him and watched her as she made shortbread on a marble block embedded in the cooking granite. I stayed on when she gave the day's menu to Bala, the cook. I walked with her when she supervised the gathering of eggs and milk, the plucking of vegetables and flowers. I watered her roses with a small tin can and walked from A to A while she baby-talked me and her flowers. After she was finished with the gouty gardener, we walked back to the house and she served us breakfast. Samir, Ma and I sat every morning on a crochet-draped dining table piled with fresh jams and marmalades with bits of peaches and strawberries and orange rinds still fresh in them. Samir then left for Hill Top Boys School in a maroon blazer and grey trousers. His hair neatly parted in two shining waves. The sun gleaming from his forehead. I wondered if he climbed to his Hill Top Boys School on a rope.

His birthday was a life-changing event for Annaville. Everything had to be rearranged. Furniture. Flowerpots. The curtains and carpets. Even the ceiling beams were polished by men on tall ladders.

Ma refused to let Anna aunty buy me a party dress, instead stitching a polka-dotted dress with a satin bow for me. But the moment I saw the strawberry lights glimmering on Annaville's pillars, I ran away. I sat outside for most of the party. Watching little girls in fruity flounces, little boys in formal and informal birthday wear and their crisply finished parents.

The guests had not yet left when Samir came out to sit on my bench with me. When we got bored of the bench, we sat on the bonnet of a guest's car and he told me about a ghost he had befriended recently. 'I saw him flying through the night. He was coming at me with a noose but I shut the window. I have a new bicycle now. I'll teach you how to ride and then we can go into the jungle and catch the ghost.

Are you cold?' I nodded and he put his birthday blazer on my knotted shoulders.

Next day in the market, he pointed out things I would have missed otherwise, 'See that pony? It is *ambling* now. If it were a little faster, it would *trot*. If it started running, it would *gallop*!' I knew Samir could teach me a lot but not what I needed to learn most. So I asked him, 'Can you teach me how to eat an egg from an egg cup? I always make a mess of it. And the forks are always so slippery ... and I always feel afraid. Sometimes of even walking into your badminton court as if it would scold me!'

He laughed loudly and hiccupped, 'You are *funny*! Imagine being scared of a badminton court! I am not scared of anything ... remember the ghost I told you about? If I saw him ... her again, I would ask about the weather or something. *Funny* girl! Actually you are not funny, you are a cartoon—a sad cartoon!'

Sometimes, I tried to understand why I always felt a hot knot, a ball of muffled pain in my chest whenever Samir said something to me. He was kind enough, as kind as he knew how to be, but I always felt lost and always hoped that he would find me.

I always felt so disembodied in the presence of happiness. Almost like the calamine bottle with cracked glass veins I found a few days later in the garden. It was empty with just a few pink scabs of dry calamine stuck to its hollows. I picked it up and just felt sad at how bereft it looked. And how it had glinted from behind a bush, hoping to be found.

I ran into the house and told Ma I wanted to go home. Anna aunty's gently frowning eyes looked at me from above the rim of tall, chilled glass of peach juice. And I wished that Ma could have Anna aunty's peach juice and sip from tall glasses of hope. I wished life was like Dorky. Harmless. Unharmed. Frisky. I wished I could give it to Ma in a bow-tied, beribboned basket. So that she could pet it for all time to come.

10

WHEN WE RETURNED, Papu was at the railway station, waiting for us. He beamed. A news crouched behind him. Peeping over his shoulder. Uncertain of how it would be greeted. We learnt that Papu had given up his job and mortgaged the house. The drawing room had been emptied of the plywood diwan and plastic chairs to make way for a loan-powered printing press. He called it Saras Prakashan, a river of words carrying all his dreams of success. With the breaking of a coconut and chanting of mantras, Saras Prakashan began to chug.

Many others followed it into our lives. Ganga Ram, a teenaged printing man from a village near Kanpur. Out-of-work compositors desperate for a job. They all settled in what used to be our drawing room to bend over sloping tables and make spelling mistakes in lead fonts. The workers spilled before us, ink cans, laughter, swear words and their lives. We learnt that Ganga Ram, tall and chocolaty, now sixteen, had married at ten, a girl of seven. They were yet to see each other after the wedding. Kewal, despite all his smiles, actually carried the grief of losing his first-born who had crawled too close to a bucket full of boiling water.

When they worked late, Ma fussed over them all with chipped cups of cardamom tea and onion paranthas. Papu worked with them, his faded blue T-shirt blotched with ink patches. He often looked at the black machine lapping up sheets of paper with its wet, coloured tongue and said, 'She is my Goddess Kali.'

Ma put an end to my bathing under the hand-pump. 'Too many men in the house,' she mumbled and shooed me towards the kitchen for my first private bath. Whenever we went past Phulkian, the biggest offset printing press in the city, we tried not to look at the shining windows, the large signboard. We all knew that we were walking past success and walking back to a single-tongued Saras Prakashan gasping for breath. To cheer us up, Papu used up the first flow of cash his Goddess Kali had earned to give me a room of my own on the first floor, with a window seat overlooking the community tap.

Papu sang through the long hours he spent in an invisible ICU trying to resuscitate his dying dream. He started printing his own newspaper, *Secular India*, when the orders for wedding cards, pamphlets and examination papers of unregistered schools began to dry up. He wrote editorials pleading with the ruling and Opposition leaders to not play games with the hardworking Punjabi. To not think of him as a voter. Or a Hindu or a Sikh.

Anna aunty smelt our struggles and sent me a big parcel, packed with a woollen poncho she had knitted herself, a few pairs of jeans that Samir had outgrown, some sweaters, a pink night suit and a dark blue maxi with butterfly sleeves.

When Papu did not pay the electricity bill, the power was cut off and a gold bangle disappeared from Ma's wrist, but it wasn't enough. Mamaji, the crumbling, old grocer from Jattanwala Chauntra came on his rheumatic legs to stand before our house. With one sheepish hand, he twisted a long, white beard and called out to Papu. 'Kakaji?'

This is how he addressed men he had seen growing up before his fading, affectionate eyes. 'Captain Saab?' he tried again to pry open the closed door behind which Papu hid. Papu who had once sat in an open jeep counting the bombs that fell around him, could not face him. So Ma opened the door to shield him from things he could neither bear nor acknowledge to be real.

Mamaji never addressed Ma by her name. He believed she was beyond commonplace names and always called her, 'Saau'. The word fit Ma like her skin. It meant that she was a good woman. Always beyond reproach. Always gentle. Always pure.

The moment he saw her, Mamaji's determination to talk about the unresolved entries in his credit register began to waver. He began to shift from one bowed leg to another. His stick began to draw apologies in the ground. His turban-wrapped old head began to sway. 'Saau . . . I wouldn't have come even today but my daughter-in-law was going through the register and she threatened me that she would come here herself and ask for money. How do I tell her that Kakaji is Captain Saab? A man of his word? That I have known his family longer than I have known her? How do I tell her about you? She doesn't know. She's too young. That's why I came.'

He fell silent. His eyes stayed buried in the ground. Ma

spoke, 'You will get your money by this evening. I give you my . . . no . . . Captain Saab's word.'

Mamaji nodded and left. The last bangle too disappeared from Ma's wrist.

Papu sang a little less now but the music in his blood could not be silenced even when, within three years, Saras Prakashan's heart began to skip beats and unsold copies of *Secular India* began to pile up under the staircase.

Papu walked us to the Shiva temple every night, filling dark, disapproving lanes with songs of his youth. When I cringed at his loud voice, he smiled, 'Never be ashamed of happiness. Never be afraid of it.'

Both he and Ma continued to slave over paint cans and bribed unpaid compositors with mint paranthas when they threatened to leave. On Saras Prakashan's last night in the house, Papu and Ma printed somebody's wedding cards till three in the morning. Ma looked drawn and Papu did not sing at all. In the morning, the machine was dragged away like a corpulent corpse, its feet leaving deep scars on the floor. Ma tried hard to polish the wounds but they never healed.

The electrical supply was cut many times and once, just before my school exams, Papu stood on a stool in the middle of the street and joined the severed wires with a tape. We could no longer afford to travel to Ambrosa to spend summer holidays because Papu was always between jobs. But poverty did not mean anything to me till Samir came to see us.

He had grown taller than his mother and his voice was gong-deep. At the sight of him at the railway station, I shivered with self-loathing in my white satin frock. Despite the peach plastic flowers Ma had stitched on its shimmering folds. The moment he got off the train like mountain breeze in caramel corduroys, with a Walkman in his hand and nutmeg specks in his eyes, my brown skin grew blotchier. A scar deepened on my knee and my hair turned limp under the sun.

I trailed behind the coolie, Anna aunty and Papu, stricken by Samir's tightly-spun bronze skin, his long limbs and languid stoop. Once in a while he turned to send me his slanting, close-mouthed smile. My misery only deepened when Papu hailed two rickshaws and helped Samir and Anna aunty into one. Till now, I had believed that we would at least hire a taxi for them or maybe they would choose to fly. They could do anything.

I smiled apologetically when Anna aunty helped Samir to arrange and rearrange his compass legs above a suitcase.

When they were comfortable, Papu piled the rest of their luggage, a big suitcase on wheels, a Chinese Checkers board, a chess box, a cane basket smelling of apples, a water bottle, a few spineless comics and a *Femina* in another rickshaw. Then Papu scooped me and placed me on top of the ungainly heap.

I looked incredulously at him but he had already kick-started his scooter and was saying, 'Just stay on top of your little mountain. No landslides okay?' I nodded, trying not to notice the grin on Samir's face. When the procession began to move with Papu in front, the guests in the middle and me at the end, Samir looked behind with wicked concern. He yelled, 'Don't topple off. But if you can't help it, take my Chinese Checkers along. It will keep you occupied till we pick you up.'

I smiled weakly and wished Papu would take the prettier route back home. I hoped we would go past the paneer tikka and chilli pickle smells of Corner Hotel. Past Capital Cinema Hall where Amitabh Bachchan's *The Great Gambler* was running. Past the straight-backed, proud Central Library. And Gandhiji's statue levitating over a hyacinth green pond. Past Greens, Patiala's only posh hotel with green, rectangular windows. Past the Kali temple with its tall, gold-tongued Goddess.

The Baradari Garden. And the rock garden with its plaster-of-Paris bathing beauty and a Japanese bridge. The pink and peach Malwa cinema hall whose Hindu owners maintained a mosque in the premises. Past Phul Theatre with its wall-sized mirror, its curving staircase, a red-carpeted snack lounge and a bathroom so clean you could eat off its floor. And past silky Mall Road with a water fountain frothing at its tail.

But Papu took the shortcut past the hardware shops, the rose garden with a few ambitious patches of struggling flowers, an open drain with a resident pig family, a tandoor where a woman sat on her haunches roasting pimply rotis with her tong fingers.

I saw it all through Samir's eyes. I smelt the open drains with his nostrils. And tried to look graceful when the rickshaws stopped and I slid down next to Dev Taya's sweet shop. Papu paid the two rickshaws and asked Dev Taya to pack curds and some ice 'for the guests'. I wished I could apologise to Samir and Anna aunty for Dev Taya's large baby-face, his stomach which was about to slide down his knees, the inverted commas of his legs, his bare, large feet, their overgrown, curly nails and the little smidgens of his life stuck in them.

Samir whispered to me, 'Why is he not wearing any pyjamas?'

I whispered back, 'He is wearing chaddis. Blue striped. Under the kurta. You can't see them, that's all.' Dev Taya smiled at me and suddenly I felt protective towards him, towards the brown squalor of his shop. I wished that Dev Taya's plain laddoos would beat the jalebis, malai pedas, cham chams and pea-stuffed kachoris in the new Bikaneri Bhujia Bhandar just across the road.

Papu handed me the curd and the ice in two plastic bags and the rickshaw pullers helped him take the luggage home. I disintegrated completely when Anna aunty and Samir entered Bakshi Ganda Singh Street. Anna aunty picked up her lacy, lemon-flavoured organdie to step over what, according to Samir, were 'digested puddings'. He counted each one, 'One . . . two . . . three. This fourth one is a jalebi. Must have come from a dog. Five . . . six . . . seven . . . these are pies. Must have come from buffalos.' His eyes took in everything: the curious women making small talk and maida vermicelli on little chauntras outside their homes; the small, dark doors, the windows that opened to nothing.

Samir was invincible. Nothing got to him. Not the small, flushless toilet on the terrace, not the hand-pump under which he bathed with relish in his shorts. I knew I belonged in my home and he did not. So I tried to compensate for all his discomforts. I waited patiently with a glass of lemon juice to greet him every afternoon when he woke up from his nap, dazed and cranky. I filled the bucket of water he would take to the toilet. And sang a gondola song from *The Great Gambler* under my breath to show him that I had a singing voice without cracks.

One day, when I climbed down the stairs wearing my blue maxi with the butterfly sleeves and a little powder dust on my neck, he looked at me intently from below, his mouth swollen with a smile. He began to teach me to play Chinese Checkers and chess. Then one night, we sat alone across a chessboard. Samir and the ivory and black pieces glowed like dangerous portents. I followed his fingers as they moved a piece from one square to another. I said, 'I don't understand.'

He tapped my nose and whispered, 'You will.' I never did. Because by next year everything had changed.

11

WHEN MA AND I went to Ambrosa next, Manna aunty's daughter Anu was there too. Smooth like whipped cream and tall like a Ming vase. She took one look at me and never looked again. She spread herself thick in the space between Samir and me, and Samir dared me silently to get past her or to get even. I could do neither. When the maids in the house gasped over Anu's long hair, her tiny waist and starlit smile, Samir turned around and looked at me with one of his eyebrows arched like a question mark. 'And what about her?' he asked one of them. The woman turned to look but I had already slid away from the room.

Samir walked Ambrosa's bazaars with Anu and bought her peaches from pavement vendors without looking back at me. We trailed behind them, Ma, Anna aunty and I, and one day, attracted perhaps by all my open hurts, a stray dog came over with an obvious intention to chew my leg. When I screamed, Anna aunty picked up a stick to shoo the dog and Ma kneeled to see the damages. My leg was intact under my maxi but I was not. I had seen Samir turn around, smile and walk on.

Whenever I was alone with Anu and Samir, their silence grew deep like a conspiracy. Watching me struggle with a fork and a spoon on the dining table, one of them would talk about India's hockey team and how it needed some new players. Sometimes Anna aunty looked up from her plate in confusion, but by then, both had rearranged their faces and were deep into another conversation detached from all of us.

When a crow entered the dining room through a ventilator, Samir watched its flight towards a pendent light. Then he chewed on something hard and said, 'This crow . . . if only it had pigtails! It would look just like . . .'

Anu grinned, 'I know who!'

'You talk too much. We're all getting disturbed,' Anna aunty said, without looking up from her plate.

'Fine, then I—*we*—will eat somewhere else,' said Samir.

He stormed out with his plate and Anu followed him.

Later that week, as I sat by myself in the veranda with my sketch book, I heard Anu call out to me loudly from the dining table, 'Van Gogh sweetheart? Could you just leave your sunflowers and come in here for a second?'

There was affection, though a little rough around the edges, in her voice, and my heart vaulted over a wall with joy. Maybe they were getting tired of shutting me out of their world. I scrambled up from the floor and ran inside.

They were both eating and looked up. 'We need some more pickle. And can you get us some rotis too?'

Before the words passed my ears to sting my eyes, I walked away from them and into the kitchen. Bala the cook was busy rolling out the dough. He gave me a smile. A lone tooth stood out like a beacon of sympathy from his dark mouth. His tong dropped two rotis in a casserole gingerly and apologetically.

Samir and Anu watched the casserole with laughter in their mouths and eyes. I left the casserole at the table and was thankful that I had reached my spot in the veranda without stumbling even once.

Anu shouted again, 'These are not good. Tell Bala to make softer ones. And you forgot to get us the pickle.'

I was walking back to them with another casserole when Anna aunty and Ma came into the room from the garden. Ma froze, but Anna aunty walked up to me and took the casserole. Samir watched a centrepiece of roses and ferns in silence.

'I was just . . .' Anu stood up with unfinished words and bits of fish clinging to her strawberry pout.

Anna aunty turned to her, 'No one gives orders in this house except me. And right now I have one for you both. Samir and you will have your meals with all of us or not at all. And you will not use your mouth for anything other than eating.'

The evening came slowly and painfully. I sat curled up in pain in a window seat, hurting till my fingertips under Ma's shawl. Then I saw Samir walking towards the house. He had Dorky on a leash, a sweater around his waist and sweat on his brow. Usually he took Anu with him for his evening walks, but today Anna aunty's words had sent her seething into her room.

He looked up and suddenly he and I were alone in the world. There was no sarcasm in his gaze. It was as if he had been caught unaware and did not have the time to feign a response. It was just one moment and then he looked away.

That night, at the dining table, I hurt my hand with a fork and heard him say through the noise that erupted in the room with my tears, 'Ma, now you know why she does not belong here.'

Anna aunty watched him and then me with a worry-creased forehead. Inder uncle said something in a stern voice but I heard only Samir. I began to spend all my time with my drawing-book and, one day, something gave way and Anu came to sit next to me. 'You poor thing,' she whispered, running her fingers through my hair. 'I don't know why . . .' she fumbled with words.

She had become a part of a war she had nothing to do with. I forgave her because she had no idea. She did not know. She and Samir were only part of the pain. Most of it was caused by the body that I cowered in. What I felt was devastation and it came from watching the untouched, dewy fragility of pink roses. I told her what had happened when Samir had come to Patiala. How our lives had veered out of control the night we played chess and what demons had followed us in the bed we had shared briefly. She was silent for a few minutes and then she got up. She said, 'You make me sick with pity. You're more twisted than I thought you were.'

When I saw Anu and Samir next, they averted their gaze. On the dining table, she clung to him like a halo, exchanged salt and pepper shakers with him, ate from his plate and, in the market, bought him T-shirts from her pocket money.

When Manna aunty arrived too to spend a few days at Annaville, Ma and I began to wish we were back in Patiala. Manna aunty and Ma had never found a way to talk to each other. She somehow always managed to convey that

Ma was not her family and now she decided to remind me as well. Her voice had put on weight just like her body and she missed no opportunity to use it.

She began to take Samir and Anu out every evening for ice-creams. She looked at me pointedly if I took a second helping at the dining table. 'Can't Veeren afford a holiday for his family?' she asked Anna aunty when Ma was within hearing distance, but not close enough to answer back.

She murmured in irritation when I touched the books on Samir's bookshelf. She brought home an expensive, new easel and rolls of drawing paper and gave them to Anu even though she did not like to draw. When Ma's sandals gave way, she complained how soon she tired of her shoes, and the next day, bought herself two new pairs.

Samir and Anu announced over the breakfast table one morning that they were trekking to Amba Devi's hill temple and we could join if we wanted to. Amba Devi was Ambrosa's mother and promised blessings to anyone who had the willpower to climb the 156 steps to her perch.

Anna aunty decided for Ma and me. We would go. Manna aunty turned to me and said, 'Why are you taking so long to finish that glass of milk? I see you wasting half of it anyway.' Then she turned to Anna aunty and said, 'I love family outings of any kind. Are you sure, Anna, that *all* of us should go?'

'You are right. All of us can't go. I am staying back,' Inder uncle said, with half a smile. Manna aunty saw the look in his eyes and promptly began to pick on her toast instead of Ma and me.

The next morning, when the mists had been soaked up by the sunlight, Anna aunty called Anu and me to her bedroom.

Spread out on her bed were two pink bell-bottoms and pink polka-dotted shirts. 'I got these stitched for you both,' she said and gave them to us. When Anu and I emerged from our rooms wearing the same outfits, Annaville fell quiet, which meant that Manna aunty was speechless. Samir looked away from us. Then he went to his room and came back with a straw hat and put it on Anu's head. 'I bought this for you yesterday,' he told her.

After breakfast we set out for Amba Devi. 'Here, hold this,' Manna aunty thrust the picnic basket in my hands. It was heavy and I tottered. Ma quietly took it from my hands. Anna aunty called out to Samir, 'Come here, son, and take this basket. This was your idea anyway.'

As the road began to unfurl, the green ridges by its sides slowly fell off into the valley and we spiralled weightlessly towards a white cone jutting out of the horizon.

Samir and Anu walked together and I looked away every time they looked back derisively. A pergola meant for tourists and pilgrims appeared on one side of the road and Anna aunty yelled to Samir and Anu, 'Stop there you two. We are tired!'

Samir and Anu opened the picnic basket and we all fished out sandwiches. Everyone sat down on the broken O of the stone benches next to the pergola except Samir and I.

I took a cotton napkin from the basket and spread it on the bench and then sat on it. He spread out on his stomach upon the grassy O between the O. He put his head between his arms, stretched out his legs behind him and grew still. Manna aunty saw me watching him and said, 'Anna, I haven't seen anyone who looks as hungry as this girl here. Her eyes eat everything. Even people.'

Anna aunty looked at me and winked. She said, 'I could say the same thing about your tongue, Manna.'

When we started walking again, I decided I would not look at Anu and Samir. I began reading the black inked rocks advertising batteries and laxatives and political slogans like 'Himachal ki Pukar . . . Shanta Kumar'. There was so much to look at: plastic flags of Congress and BJP candidates sticking out of bony mountainsides, garlanding balconies, fluttering on slate roofs; little children waving to us from windows; shops that offered sticky, sweet and sour aam paapads, dahi vadas and karhi chawal.

Anu walked with a transistor in her hand. '*Is mod se jaate hain*,' she sang with Lata Mangeshkar and Kishore Kumar. Even though she claimed it, I felt it was my song. I imagined I was alone in the valley and climbing up a steep road to something benevolent and loving.

The stone steps appeared in a distance. A few discontented flower-sellers sat in a knot by one side with untouched mounds of marigolds. Their day had obviously begun badly. They brightened up when Anna aunty went from one mound to another, picking up garlands for us all. On the twenty-fifth step, Manna aunty exploded at me, 'I can't trouble myself for your whims.'

Everyone knew that I was just an incidental victim and that she had just wanted to vent so the transistor was left behind to keep her company and we went on. Anna aunty bought a leaf platter heaped with halwa for the Goddess from a vendor at the mouth of the temple. The temple had a conical, slate roof but no walls. A pre-historic stone stood in the middle. The Goddess had emerged from it, birthed Ambrosa and then disappeared into it. Her pet lion stood next to it. We fed him the halwa and it disappeared in his stone belly. 'The same halwa will now be given back to the vendor who will sell it again to fools like us,' Samir whispered to Anu. Anna aunty glared at him and we walked out from the temple and stood in the balcony overlooking the town.

For a minute, all of us stood in silence, looking at the miniature painting of Ambrosa. 'That is "Perfect Eight",' Samir whispered. I knew it was me he was talking to. I followed his gaze to see the grey silk ribbon twisted in two perfect halves and the liquid band of Chawli, the massed up darkness of pines, the red roof and white walls of Annaville, the paddy cakes and the sloping tea-gardens.

We were all quiet on the way home. Manna aunty joined us with complaints about how the hot stairs had skinned her bottom. My calves hurt but I walked lightly. The goddess had left her stone and come with me. When we reached Annaville's gate, I noticed Anu's bell-bottoms. They were streaked with tiny little mud blotches. I didn't have to look down to know that there was not a speck of dust on mine. I had survived the trek without any scars.

12

THE NEXT DAY, Inder uncle proposed a picnic to Panchel, a small velvety patch a few miles away from Ambrosa. Ma spent an entire day stitching a khaki skirt I could wear with a cheese-cotton top on the trip. On the morning of the picnic, I wore it and stepped out in the sunshine and heard Manna aunty laugh, 'My God! See what we have! Brown hair, a brown face and a brown skirt. Perfect colour-coordination!'

'Aah, the burnt toast she insisted upon eating every morning when she was five,' Anna aunty smiled.

'Burnt toast? When did I have it? You remember the strangest things! And what has that got to do with anything?' fumed Manna aunty.

'With sour curd on the side!'

'So?'

'So.'

'Meaning?'

Now Inder uncle interrupted the two sisters, one pink with mischief, the other almost red with rage, 'Aftertaste,

Manna, aftertaste. It has lasted pretty long. Too long if you ask me. Now let me just end this ridiculous conversation right here and hire a van since Tek Singh and his apprentice have chosen to fall sick together.'

The van came but the journey seemed predestined for disaster. Anu and Samir of the 'entertainment committee' brought along a tape recorder but forgot all about fresh batteries. The old ones, they discovered, had died a quiet and powdery death, and an argument between the two erupted about who should have known better.

Manna aunty, fidgeting to sit next to Ma and to destroy her with her silence, found herself seated next to Inder uncle, who destroyed her with his silence, his reading glasses and a Robert Ludlum thriller. She turned her face away from everything and watched the hill-scapes with hot, angry eyes. Ma and Anna aunty sat behind her and immediately forgot all about her.

I sat alone next to a window and did not watch either Anu or Samir. They noticed it and did not know what to talk about, now that their batteries were dead and a slain foe had somehow risen and walked away. Samir scowled and chewed on his Mintis. Anu stared hard at a film magazine.

Then, of course, the van coughed and broke down. In the middle of a place where nothing could be repaired ever. We got down and stepped on a brown wrinkle of an old, beaten mountain. A few Gaddi tribals looked at us pityingly as they sheared their sheep in a green hollow. An injured water pipe spurted out water helplessly above a rock. We only had dung mounds, old, dusty pine cones, empty pouches of paan masala and each other for company.

The driver tinkered with the engine but nothing came to life. Then Inder uncle waved a local bus to a stop and we got on. The bus reeked of goats, tobacco, old vomit and farmers from small villages on their way to Panchel's vegetable market. Badly-sewn potato sacks sat on seats and tottered in the aisles. There were many school children too, swaying and squealing with every turn the bus took.

There were many hooked noses and umbrellas in the bus and the bus conductor was patient with both but he saved his broadest smile for Inder uncle. 'What maharaj? Off for a peeknic? Private van died? At least we know how to repair our buses, sir. Or if we can't, we have another bus to take care of the passengers. Anyway, most welcome to all of you all.'

After making sure that tickets had been bought for us, the bus conductor went about arranging us in the bus. Soon Samir was sitting on a sack of potatoes. Anu next to two women and a baby. She turned away and made a face when one woman took out a weathered leather teat to shove it into the baby's mewling mouth.

Two men vacated their seat to accommodate Anna aunty, Ma and me. Manna aunty found a sliver at the back of the bus to settle her bitterness down. I sat on Ma's lap and Inder uncle was escorted by the conductor 'personally' to his own 'personal' seat.

No one talked much. Samir held on to our seat whenever the potatoes under him got restive. During a quieter moment when nothing moved in the bus except the trees outside its windows, Samir took out a mint from his jacket and offered it to me. I took it and looked away from him. It was too soon. And I knew that now I needed to look away every time he looked at me.

Twenty minutes later, we got down from the bus and I tried not to see the yellow spattered part of the bus where someone leaning from a window had rid himself of a vile breakfast. Everything else looked clean. In the bright day, Harigiri stood in naked hauteur, and Panchel was a rippling carpet. Right at its centre, there was a glass lake cradling an island.

'This island is a miracle. It moves from one place to another but no one can see it moving,' Inder uncle told me. I looked at the island and it looked at me. It was my mirror image. I knew then that, one day, I would move away to a place no one ever expected me to reach. The thought made everything else easier to bear. Especially the sight of Anu and Samir playing around with a picnic basket, trying to wrench it from each other, running towards waiting ponies.

I suddenly missed Papu and wanted to be back in Patiala with him. He had always laughed and sang through deprivations and I was his daughter. I let his joy and strength flood my veins and decided that Samir would never know how much he had hurt me. By seeking me out. By rejecting me. By marking me on a night that had begun with a bright and safe morning.

Papu had taken Samir and me to the green house near Baradari Garden. It glittered like a giant, filigreed cage with little green things trapped inside it. We walked around dark, teeming plants that nodded hungrily for company. Papu stayed outside talking to college friend who had hollered at him from across the road. The two were busy back-slapping each other.

An old man walked up to Samir and me and asked, 'You want some rain? I can make some if you want.' Samir and

I looked at each other with large eyes and in a minute, a cloud-burst exploded in our cage. Samir took both my hands and swirled me around. I whirled deliriously, my face raised to the rain. I didn't know my skin was so parched. I felt like one of the plants. Happy to drink the downpour. Sated till my roots.

Then the rain stopped. We did too but my mind was still a whirlpool. When I opened my eyes, Samir was gone. I stood alone, shivering in a wet frock that clung to my body. To breasts I had never noticed before.

In the evening, we took a bus to Sanaur to spend the night at a farmhouse that Ashok uncle, one of Papu's college friends, had just built. He had recently joined a political party and aspired to be a member of parliament at some point of his life.

He came to the Sanaur bus-stop to meet us, wearing a khadi kurta in respectful deference to his allegiance to Gandhian ideals. He stuffed us all in his Ambassador and drove us through the sugarcane fields of his father to a house that seemed to have been made out of wet, dripping chocolate pudding. The drawing room had a high ceiling and poster-sized photos of his brand-new son. 'The sofas? From foreign embassy auctions in Delhi,' he informed Papu. The sofas were covered with home-embroidered panels. The walls were a proud pink and studded with his photographs with political leaders.

'See the bar, Veeren? All imported maal,' he said, walking on discordant carpets. An overpowering smell of tandoori chicken floated all around us. His wife, a thin, dark woman, hugged Ma and Anna aunty and escorted us all out to the backyard where a bonfire was crackling. Sugarcanes swayed in the night for miles around us and rustled strangely as if someone was mussing them up.

Papu and Ashok uncle settled down on a charpoy with a plate of kebabs between them. 'And I said to the party president, give me an election ticket. I will get you all the Hindu votes from Patiala,' Ashok uncle was saying between chicken bites. Papu swayed his head but said nothing and they drank from glinting cut-glasses and clinked them whenever there was a pause in the conversation.

The rest of us had chairs to ourselves, and a table laid out with plates and saag, roti, chutney and raita. Samir was unusually quiet and refused to sit next to me, choosing instead to sit on the veranda steps with his walkman.

'What happened, did you two fight?' Anna aunty asked. I shook my head. Everyone forgot about us when the baby was brought out in a pram. Samir ate alone on the steps.

'I will sleep outside,' he told Anna aunty sullenly when it was time for us to go to our rooms. I changed into my nightclothes in the room I was to share with Ma and Papu. 'I don't want to sleep now,' I told Papu and ran down the stairs to see where Samir intended to sleep.

His overnight bag was open. His chessboard lay next to it, but he was not to be seen anywhere. Then I saw him emerging from a bathroom at the end of the veranda. He was dressed in white drawstring slacks and a blue T-shirt.

He looked at me coldly and passed me by to go to the charpoy. A mattress, pillows and bed sheets had been piled on it and he began making his bed. I sat down on the veranda steps to watch him.

When he pulled a sheet to his neck and turned his back on me, I said, 'I'm not feeling sleepy. I'm bored and you didn't play chess with me today.'

He turned to face me and propped himself up on an arm. He smiled just a bit, 'You want to play?'

I nodded. We put the chessboard on a table in the veranda and pulled two stools close to it. The whole house was dark by now and the bonfire had turned pink and flat.

I could not focus on anything except the way his slim, brown hands moved on the chessboard. When my eyes began to blur, I confessed to him how little of chess I understood. I knew I would remember the way he tapped my nose and said, 'You will.' Then he said, 'Enough,' and we both scrambled up.

I smiled a good-night at him and then said, 'I don't want to go.'

'Stay,' he said.

'Okay,' I said simply and climbed into his bed. I tucked myself in his bed sheet, turned my back to him and closed my eyes. Then I felt his breath in my hair.

The sugarcanes wheezed and hissed and the night felt vast and cold on my skin. I shivered. I felt his hand on my back and turned my head just a bit to look at him. His eyes were half-open with a smile.

I turned away and closed my eyes. The bonfire was almost dead but I felt the warmth of its last surviving embers on the nape of my neck.

The sugarcanes became the pine trees of Ambrosa and a Sun God walked out of the groves and I felt him just behind me. His warm, liquid fingers flickered slowly on my back. Samir was quiet. So was I. The night was our womb and we looked at the same darkness and the same stars. Turning just a bit to look at him, I fumbled clumsily, and managed to reach a few buttons on the back of the pink night suit given to me by Anna aunty and felt his hand again. Slowly, deliberately, unbuttoning it.

I glanced at him but could not look for long. He was too beautiful. His eyes were barely open. He smiled dangerously. As if he were on the brink of destroying everything in sight.

Slowly, life seeped out of me. I grew empty. I was not Papu's daughter anymore. I was nothing. I was an ivory piece in Samir's hands and he would soon move me to a new, forbidden square. I was older than my thirteen years.

I was some strange, dark woman Samir had known forever. And this woman was a valley of hunger. She was eager to touch him; to see if his skin was made of sunbeams, or moonlight. She wondered what would happen if she turned to face him. If she buried her face in his neck and let his warmth melt on every inch of her darkness. If her mouth touched his.

Then I was Ma and I stood on a ledge. I could see nothing. Everything was dark and yielding. And then I was a girl who could feel nothing except two curious hands searching for some unspeakable answer from her body.

I flinched when the hands wilfully, persuasively broke through untouched barriers, to indent a part of me which I had not even known the existence of.

Suddenly a window grew yellow with a snap in the first floor. And then I was stabbed by loathing. For Samir, for what his hands had been trying to find. And for myself, because I knew then without a shade of doubt that I loved him and that the revulsion rising from my bitter, convulsing stomach was nothing. It would pass, but I would come back once again to Samir.

When the loathing turned into tears, I got out of the bed

and ran to Papu. Even after Samir left, I continued to seethe in shame and pain. His hands became part of a cosmic puzzle. Had they touched me because I was open to defilement? Or because there was something confounding between us? At school, I grew quiet and sullen and wondered how girls could swing their legs from desks and speak to young boys with young and eager smiles.

When I met Samir again at Annaville, I discovered how hard it was to disown love that ran like poison in my blood. I knew I would shudder for years at the memory of undressing in Annaville's guest room and his walking in, just in time to see me duck behind the bed. I knew I would shiver with shame at the memory of his words when he picked up a book from the cabinet, stopped at the door and said, 'I am not interested in looking at you.'

I wished at times to change my skin, wash away the ugliness crawling on my bones and win his sunlight back. I wandered into his bathroom and buried my face into his shirt to smell the fragrance that banished all my pain, all my hurt. I touched his jeans on the clothesline and felt comforted. I dreamt of Samir and woke up wondering what would have happened if I hadn't run away that night. Would I have found something? Lost something? Why had I felt violated by his hands when he was Samir and had ruled my world forever?

But I knew that I could not have stayed. My spirit was like Papu's. It did not welcome intrusion.

Panchel healed me partially. I shut all my pain along with my shame in a box where a few teenagers were putting away little tadpoles. I did not seek Samir for the rest of the day. I sat in the train with Ma to go back to Papu and

Patiala, and knew then that one day he would lose the power to hurt me or reach me. I imagined myself in denim overalls, my hair twisted around small beads, my mouth glistening like a coffee-bean, my eyes clear and bright and my laughter rippling like silk in a world impervious to him.

13

WHEN WE GOT back, Ma joined a private school as a temporary teacher.

A letter from Delhi informed us that Naren uncle had sent his son to Muscat and suddenly and inexplicably made a fortune out of this decision. His wife came to visit us with years of repressed emotions glittering like diamonds on her, 'We have bought a new car. Could not bring here. It is parked in the Fort. Driver is sleeping in the car. No parking place in your Bakshi Ganda Singh Street, Captain Veeren.'

'We don't need cars in a small town like ours. Sometimes, we use rickshaws and occasionally, we use our imagination to get from one place to another,' Papu said, trying very hard to suppress a grin.

When lunch was served, Nimmo aunty loudly sighed, 'Aah, lunch is ready but I can't eat this rice. I only eat basmati now. Anything cheaper gives me acidity.'

'Rani, no lunch for Nimmoji . . . only an antacid,' Papu said as Ma tried to hush him.

I had stayed in my room for the most part of her visit and

smiled detachedly at her as we all sat down to eat.

Spoon suspended in mid-air, she ran her eyes over the batik skirt Anna aunty had sent me recently and said, 'What are you wearing, little girl? Wasn't this in fashion two years ago? Your cousin Mona has so many clothes now, she can't close her wardrobe door.'

'I won't have the same problem aunty, because our wardrobes don't have doors and I'm not very interested in clothes,' I said as Ma threw up her hands.

Nimmo aunty continued as if she had not heard me, 'You must come and see our house. We have marble flooring all over. Bittu has four speakers for his music-system. Two on the wall. Two on the side tables.'

'Four? I thought, there was only one loud speaker in that house!' Papu said under his breath.

After lunch, she brought out a packet and said to me, 'Here. A wraparound skirt for you girl. Do you know how to wear it? Also try these shoes my Bittu got from Dubai. Didn't fit Mona or me. You can have them but do you know how to walk on high-heels? You know, one must look presentable at all times. Why, even my servants are dressed better than some people I know. It is a question of class. You either have it or you don't.'

I looked inside the bag and said, 'One can't walk on high heels in these mohallas aunty, so no high heels for me. And the skirt . . . seems too classy for me. Maybe one of your servants can wear it.'

This hit her hard and she grew almost orange with rage, 'Do you know how to cook? No? Why is no one teaching you? And why are you always shut in your room? Who do you think you are going to be?'

I opened my mouth to speak but Ma signalled frantically at me to shut up, so I did.

Nimmo aunty rolled on, 'Mona will be ready for marriage in a few years. I am already buying kundan jewellery for her. You just wait and see how I marry her off. Your brother is just like you, Veerenji. Never did much for his family. It is God's grace that I have come so far in life. My daughter is lucky to have a brother who can buy anything she wants now without looking at the price-tags.'

After she was spent, she went back to her newly prosperous abode. And fate changed Ma's life in a swift decision. One day, as she trudged down the road to catch a bus to her school, she was hit by a truck and flung off the road. There was no parachute this time to bail her out and so she flew without wings and did not know how to land. But sometimes prayers too become parachutes. And so when she was sinking, a jeep stopped near her and a man jumped out. Two hours later, when Papu and I ran through Rajindra Hospital's long, pungent corridors to find her, that man— his shirt smeared till the collars in Ma's blood—met us near the emergency ward. He gave us a few sugar batashas. 'Before you came, I went to the dargah near Sanaur. I believe in the peer whose spirit lives there. I promised him a chadar if he watches over her. When she is able to walk, we will take her to him.'

Papu nodded. So the peer, Papu's resilience and the faith of Ma's rescuer fought for Ma. First in the emergency room where she was opened, sealed and bandaged and then in the general ward where she bobbed between pain and drugged sleep and called for 'Amma' and 'Papaji'. Papu became aware of Ma in a way he had never been. It was almost as if she had been X-rayed, blown up and plastered on the world's walls. Now that she could not speak, he heard everything. The way her blood roared in her veins and the way her heart pulsed. He checked all her medical charts and somehow guessed that her damaged liver was insidiously bleeding inside her. He got the taciturn Dr Jolly Singh to unsew her and stitch up the fissure from where blood was quietly, dreadfully oozing.

Papu made a ceremony out of our walks down the long, chilly corridor out of general ward. He talked a lot, laughed a lot, and then at the gate of the hospital fed me gobhi paranthas with fat chunks of pickled mango and butter from a little dhaba.

A thick stream of Ma's well-wishers began to gush into her ward. Soma, the cleaning woman came. So did Mamaji, the grocer, with a thermos of goat liver soup because Ma had suffered liver injuries. Papu's old compositors and machine men came and sat next to her and laughed about the many midnights of printing frenzy when she had to cook post-dinner-pre-breakfast meals for them.

In a few weeks Ma was ready to come home. Her soft, shining hair had been matted with blood for weeks and not been washed properly by the hospital nurses. 'Buy me a nice-smelling shampoo,' was the first thing she said when Papu seated her in a taxi.

Anna aunty had sent us all the money we needed to get Ma back and she was home to open the door for us. She and Papu settled Ma, and Papu put on a Jagjit Singh cassette on the second-hand tape recorder he had bought. 'He's a Sikh. He looks like a Hindu. He sings like a Sufi poet. You will love him,' he told Ma. Then he sang along with the ghazal, '*Kal chowdhavi ki raat thi ... shab bhar raha charcha tera ... kucch ne kaha ye chaand hai ... kucch ne kaha chehra tera.*' Last night in the light of the full moon, there was talk only of you. Some called the moon by its name and others said it was your face.

Then Anna aunty soaked Ma's hair in a tub of warm water, covered the knots with a gentle oil and massaged in the shampoo. When the last jasmine bubble had been washed away, she towelled Ma's hair and chopped it till her ears. Anna aunty left in a couple of days but Papu continued to guard Ma's life with fearful passion and she began to glow with a quiet happiness though it was tinged with a vague fear. This fear became a living beast the day she was alone in the house and heard footsteps coming down from the terrace towards her room.

She crouched uselessly under a sweaty sheet till the footsteps stopped about five feet from her. When there was no sound for a few minutes, she dared to look at the doorway. A man stood there, and she instinctively knew that he had no living blood. He seemed to have survived a carnage somewhere and blood ran across his face and drenched his tattered clothes. 'You survived this too, did you?' he rasped at her, his large, bulging eyes pinning her down with their hatred.

'You have always escaped, haven't you? Let me see how far will you run,' he whispered and turned away to go where he had come from. Ma felt the house caving in on her and when she opened her eyes again, Papu was holding her tight and a doctor was rubbing with cotton, the needle prick on her numb wrist.

Ma recovered unwillingly now. Slowly and tediously. She

began to feel that something had followed her across the border, to stalk, hunt and kill all over again. When terrorist attacks on buses began to monopolise newspaper headlines, her nightmares returned.

The argument of this terror was different from the one that had claimed her childhood, but the Punjab she had come to love grew bloodier everyday and the blood belonged to everyone. Hindus, Sikhs, the ones who didn't know that they were supposed to know the difference.

Manek, a young medical representative we knew, was shot dead while visiting village dispensaries on his faithful scooter. That day, he was riding past a sugarcane field when a gun shot sent him rolling on the road. His scooter lay screaming on its hide but Manek quietly bled to death.

'Don't be afraid,' Papu told Ma. 'It's just a fever. Just a few people who can't see they are shedding their own blood. Punjab will never fall to them. It cannot be divided. We will have to worry only when ordinary people like us get infected by this slow-spreading, fast-rising fever. When our neighbours join the mob, only then will we have to worry.'

And then one night, the mob came home. Ma had been trying to sleep during a hot summer night and Papu was helping me finish my home-work when the door trembled under quick, furtive knocks. Papu opened the door and I recognised Swarna, the Hindu typist who was a tenant in a Sikh home.

'Veerji! They will kill me,' she panted between sobs as Papu shut the door behind her.

'What happened?' Papu sat her down next to Ma's bed.

'He, my landlord, didn't want Bunty . . . my boyfriend

. . . to come home and meet me. Last night, we were at Phul Theatre with a few friends, watching a film, and we saw the landlord and his wife a few rows away. After the show, Bunty and his friends beat up the man and tore his wife's dupatta. When the man began to bleed, Bunty panicked and ran away. I came back home because I had nowhere else to go. The family did not realise I was back because everyone was at the hospital. Then the women came. They dragged me out and beat me. I ran. I came to you. I don't know why.'

Ma looked at her and said the only unkind words I ever heard her say. 'I think you should go out and let them tear you to pieces. I don't want anybody at my door again with blood in their eyes. *Ever*. You got that? Now get out.'

Papu put his finger on his lips because there was a rumble in the lane outside. Ma clutched her bedside and Papu sat me down next to her and put her hand in mine. The woman huddled in a corner and her body rocked to and fro and screamed noiselessly.

Papu looked at Ma and me and went away. I knew that he had opened the door and locked it behind him when I heard the click of a key. I had to see what was going on; I ran to the terrace and looked down. Papu was facing a crowd that consisted of his Sikh playmates, their young sons, women and something that was not hatred but an ancient bonhomie splintered by a sudden mistrust.

'I can't hand over the woman to you,' he was telling the wife of the battered man. She was leading the crowd and I saw her kirpan shiver in the moonlight.

The woman chewed each one of her words, 'Veeren, I have no argument with you. Nobody has ever had any argument with you. This is not about Hindus and Sikhs. This is about justice. And teaching a lesson to anyone who crosses a boundary. She crossed all boundaries. I have fed her the food I cooked for my children. I just didn't want her polluting my girls with that dog who came every night to hump her. That was all. She stood and watched while he and his friends broke my husband's bones. She will pay with her blood. I won't kill her Veeren, but if you stop me, I will kill you,' the woman said and inched a little closer to what seemed to me the end of everything.

Papu did not move an inch. In a voice that caressed the night with its smile, he said, 'I can't give you the key, sister. When I can't stand anymore to guard this door, you can go inside. Break me down first and then the door. Then you can kill the woman. And my wife and daughter too. Will that satisfy you? Or heal your man any faster? I won't hand over the woman to you, not because she is right and you are wrong, but because you cannot set anything right by another wrong. Go home. Throw her things out of your house. Wash your hands off her and blight her with your curses. But if you do to her what she did to you, someone else will step in to avenge her and then our children will pay for our impatience. Forgive her. Don't make a mistake that life will never let you forget.'

The woman began to cry. 'I want to cut her to pieces, Veeren. I have nothing against you. Don't force me to do something I don't want to do.' She slouched down to the ground. I saw Papu crouch next to her and the stiff crowd began to soften. I came down and told Ma that Papu would be fine. It was dawn when we heard receding footsteps and the reassuring click in the lock.

Papu came inside and said to the girl shivering under a blanket that Ma had given her. 'Make yourself a cup of tea in the kitchen and quietly leave. As long as you don't show your face in this neighbourhood, you will be fine.' The woman shook as she got up and went away.

14

THE NEXT DAY, the news spread that death had come to
our doorstep, sniffed at its inmates and retreated. By evening,
the house was filled with shining trishuls and Hindu anger.
Papu looked more agitated than he had the previous night.
He asked me to fetch water for the young boys sitting
around him. Then he spoke, 'Why do you want to set fire
to their homes? Do you know that all the houses in this
neighbourhood have common walls? If you set fire to one
house, the next ten houses will burn. This one too. And I
will tell you this. Last night, when they stood outside my
door, I did not fear them. Not for one moment. I knew my
life was in safe hands. But if you do anything foolish,
neither Hindus nor Sikhs will feel safe living next to each
other. I owe it to my daughter and their children to never
let that happen.'

The boys went away but not before their presence was
heard and seen by the entire Jattan Walla Chauntra. Later
that night, I was reading in the drawing room. Ma and
Papu were sleeping as usual in the next room because she

was still too weak to climb the stairs to her bedroom. It was close to midnight when I switched off the light and stretched out on the diwan and tried to sleep. It was dark around me but still the room seemed bright. I lay for some time, watching the strange light in the room and then sprang to my feet. The light was flickering and it smelt of kerosene.

I opened the drawing room door and went near the hand-pump where Papu's scooter was hauled up and parked each night. I looked at the door that opened into the street and then my eye travelled to small snakes of fire writhing at its bottom edge, itching to enter the house and to destroy everything.

I walked up to Papu and Ma and whispered, 'Papu, the house is on fire.' Before I could finish my sentence, Papu was on his feet and bounding towards the hand-pump. I began to pump water in the buckets. Papu threw the door open and a cloud of fire came inside. He doused most of it with a splash of water and then stood transfixed when he saw Ma, her tinctured gown stuck to her bandaged stomach, attacking the fire with a wet towel.

We worked silently and, within minutes, the fire was just a wet sandbag reeking of kerosene. Papu carried Ma to her bed, wiped her sweat and came back into the street and shouted. The loudest he ever had. 'This house is not an island. Its windows look into yours, its walls are yours too. Then why?'

The woman who had picketed around our house opened her door and came out, 'I swear on everything I hold sacred to me Veeren, this was not done by us. If you can believe me, I will be relieved. If not, we will have to accept that we can no longer live on the same soil without drawing blood.'

Papu looked at her and said, 'I believe you.'

We never learnt who had set fire to the house, but after that moment, the neighbours, both Hindus and Sikhs, decided to watch over each other's homes with lanterns, kirpans and lathis at night. They stayed awake on their terraces and, at the slightest sound, alerted each other with loud cries. Sometimes they heard the sounds of receding feet and sometimes they heard nothing but the night.

Ma now began to recover fast. Her hair grew back and the stitches on her stomach healed, leaving behind just a plump, brown caterpillar. Habitual pain visited her but was wounded every time because now Papu shooed it away. He had always given her love. Now he gave her a life blessed by a monthly pay-cheque. He stuck to his marketing job in a biscuit company despite being reminded by his boss that his grandfather did not own the office and that he needed to cultivate humility.

Ma had taken too little from life and Papu had always taken too much. Now he repaid many of his debts. He tore down a few mouldy walls, whitewashed and smoothened the rest and poured light in dark corners. He built her a cooking platform in the kitchen and a bathroom bigger than the kitchen. It had a duco-painted wooden cabinet, a giant geyser, a shining mosaic floor, a pristine white sink and Western-style commode. He bought her a cherry-red, rexine sofa, a colour television, a second-hand fridge, a two-in-one music system, a Japanese mixie, a double-burner gas stove, a couple of beige and off-white curtains, floral night-dresses, imported sarees, a jute owl for one wall, a mounted poster which said, 'You only live once but if you live right, once is enough'. He even got a motor fitted in the hand-pump.

I was doing well in school and had a few trophies to show for it. My school walls were crowded with my paintings and I was asked to paint backdrops and props for dance ensembles and plays and given sawdust and coloured powders to make rangoli designs at the gate to welcome the chief guest during the annual fete. Papu bought stacks of greeting cards from my stall and told acquaintances that I had designed the time-table for my classroom. He bought me a drawing board and sent me to inter-school drawing contests to conquer the world.

And I did. I went again and again to the school stage during the annual function, dressed in a grown-up sari and dabs of rouge to collect prizes for my singing, for my 'original' drawings showing Papu shaving in his pyjamas next to a crumpled Old Spice tube. For poetry recitation and story-telling. I was the pride of Ashoka House and despite my embarrassing scores in Mathematics, my teachers made it clear that they believed I was going somewhere very special because I could speak passionately on stage against terrorism with Kaifi thrown in as a punchline:

Aaj ki raat bahut garam hawa chalti hai
Aaj ki raat na neend aayegi
Hum sub uthen, main bhi uthun, tum bhi utho
Koi khidki isi deewar mein khul jayegi

Tonight, the wind is scalding / tonight, there will be no sleep / we must rise, me and you / and then one day, a window will open in the wall before us.

When it was time again to visit Ambrosa, I had no diffidence.

Ma and I took the night train to Ambrosa from Asankot, and from my train window, it looked like a cluster of fireflies. The moon glistened like a freshly wiped mirror. I knew this time I would step on Annaville's flower-fringed, rain-splashed stone steps with a whole soul. Not like a leper crouching before the full-bodied. I promised myself I wouldn't feel ugly and misshapen even if Samir looked up at me from the bottom of the steps with a badly concealed smirk. This time it would be different. I was no longer afraid of his peak caps, his denim jackets, his scorching laughter, his spicy perfumes, his stacks of books and his power over me.

I no longer felt poor. Even in the faded jeans that Samir had outgrown and Anna aunty had sent to me in a parcel, I felt slender and fragrant. I knew my eyes looked squarely at everything. My hair skimmed my waist and acquired a life of its own on breezy days. My wrists were thin but strong. Capable of painting anything at all. My taut brown skin was sealed against injuries now.

The station hummed with lights and trees and a gentle rain. As our taxi sped towards Annaville, I realised I was no longer alone. Someone much older than my fifteen years lived within me and would now take care of the girl who fumbled with forks and could not rebut slights. When the taxi stopped, I stepped into something sacred. A moment that I knew would change my life forever and would bring me face-to-face with something unknown and unknowable. A moment that, despite all its strange magic, was as familiar as Annaville's freshly-watered roses.

15

ANNA AUNTY WAS in the veranda and threw her arms wide open for Ma and me. Her garden smelt of full-blown spring and wet earth. Plump orange buds rioted like always around the pillars, and the sky was ablaze with stars.

I knew Samir was behind a screened door, looking at us, before he came out to meet us. I did not need to look at him. I knew that gait, that stoop, from a previous life.

There were a few new things in the drawing room. I picked up a blue urn I had never seen before and put it back on the mantelpiece among spiralling gold candles and silver photo frames, one of which contained a photograph of Dorky. He had died the previous year. There was a picture of Samir and me too. He was perhaps three, I, one. He was scowling at me and I was busy licking a messy lolly. My curls were all over the picture and my frock was made up of marzipan frills.

'This was taken in Kanpur but you would not remember,' said Anna aunty. I turned away from the picture to find Samir looking at me. He turned away quickly but not before giving himself away. There was surprise in his eyes. 'Samir is studying hard. He was a school prefect and now has to live up to himself in college, you see,' Anna aunty laughed as she piled snowy, white pillows on my bed.

Inder uncle had recently set up a tea factory in Ambrosa and was away in Calcutta for a tea auction. Anna aunty and Ma had decided to stay up all night in the master bedroom to talk. She switched off all the lights and said, 'You don't need a night-lamp, do you? You will be disturbed by the light in Samir's room anyway.'

She left me sheathed in happiness. Samir's room across the corridor was a fluorescent slit in the dark. I continued to replay Samir's gaze in my mind, till a smelly train compartment, an old man snivelling into a snuff box, red-and-brown coolies, orange buds and a black-and-white Samir collided with each other and fell into darkness.

I dreamt I was on a boat; it swayed every time I took a breath. I realised how alone I had been when I saw another boat. It was just a gray hulk and it moved stealthily towards me. Someone was on that boat. Then a torchlight cut through swathes of the night and reached me. I woke up. Samir's door was ajar and dimly-lit by a fiery red ember. The ember looked like a hand. It was masking the bare face of a torch. Trying to cut out the beam that had been searching for me. I turned my back on Samir's tortured curiosity and went to sleep.

I woke up to a morning that was still just a rustle, just a whisper. The sun was not yet ripe and the garden was painted in rosy shadows. Everything was liquid like a perfect Chinese water-colour and I blurred like a drop in it. I sat down on a stone bench under a ruffled arch of pink petals. The grass-bordered stone pathway under my feet was damp and cold. Under the morning shower of dew and leaves shed by the silver oaks, I felt one with an earth drenched with joy.

And something whispered to me that nothing was denied and everything was mine if only I could reach out to claim it.

During the next few days, Samir hovered around me cluelessly. Not knowing what was the right thing to say or do. He laughed too loudly. Sometimes played home movies where he posed dramatically against cliffs and sunsets and asked no one in particular, 'I think someone we know looks very handsome here! Or am I flattering myself too much? The suspense is killing me!'

When I laughed at something, he would ask, 'And the joke is?' If I was too quiet, he said, 'What happened to the weather Ma? It's very dark and gloomy out here.'

At times he strolled to the dining table for breakfast, wearing a vest that showed off his newly-developed muscles and flexing his arms till Anna aunty firmly asked him to get lost and get dressed. He sang *Strangers in the Night* in the large, empty house when Ma and Anna aunty strolled in the garden and I shut the main door, loudly enough for him to hear, and walked out in the veranda. I took phone messages from breathless girls and passed them on to him with a smile, while he searched my face for a flicker of pain. I brought a tray of cookies and a teapot to his room when a girl, smelling of lime-blossoms and warm sweat, came to visit him and sat in front of him, running her nervous fingers through her hair. When he dressed in silk shirts, sprayed a tangy cologne all over himself and left on his bike to meet 'someone special', I did not let it hurt me.

I sat in my favourite window-seat with a book one evening when I saw him enter the drawing room and walk straight to the chest-of-drawers to pick up the ornate phone. He dialled, reciting the number out aloud, and began to talk to someone in a flirtatious, caressing, teasing voice. 'How can anyone ever forget you?' he whispered loudly into the phone.

I could not will my eyes to stay away from him. They left the words swimming in the book and looked at him. He stood with his legs crossed, one hand holding the phone and the other drumming the chest of drawers. His eyes were intent. They were watching me. I turned back to my book. When I looked up again, he had turned his back.

I did not know what I wanted him to say to me. I knew though that there was more to us than just the games he played with me. The game of showing me that he wanted me but never to the point of helplessness. The game of trying to show me how irrevocably I was branded by him. And that there would never be another man as much a part of me as he was.

I knew that we were part of a big, beautiful and as yet unarticulated truth and that, if he continued to turn his back on it, one day, he would find me gone from his life and never find me again.

One evening, Anna aunty coaxed Samir to join us for a walk. We were somewhere in the middle of Perfect Eight, when clouds began to swell in the sky. 'Such a clear sky when we started,' Anna aunty frowned. We began to walk fast but the storm pushed us with wet, powerful knuckles to the edge of the road.

'Run,' Samir shouted above the din.

Anna aunty held on to Samir. Ma and I held each other. We saw nothing because the sun had been doused out. 'Get in there,' Samir pointed at a tourist pergola. We stumbled in. Ma and Anna aunty sat down on a bench, giggling like young girls over the squelches made by their bottoms. I joined them. Samir stood behind Anna aunty, his arms around her neck.

'Look,' he pointed at the road, leaning over her. Hailstones were fast piling up in pearly heaps around Perfect Eight. I shivered with joy and instinctively turned towards Samir to see that he had been watching me, not the rain.

When Ma and I left Ambrosa, Samir was altered in a way even he could not really conceal. There was a frank respect in his eyes, an acknowledgement that he had been wrong. About something. About my vulnerability. And, perhaps, his invulnerability.

16

DURING MY LAST year in school, the silence between us was broken. Samir's letters began to wander into my tin letter-box like stray leaves from afar. The letters were brief and cryptic to begin with. Watchful, mildly curious.

'I don't even know which class you are in!'

'What do you do with your time? I do remember that you paint . . . do you still paint?'

'I read your letters to Ma (Sorry! But sometimes, when she is busy in the kitchen, she wants me to read her your letters because they really are epics! I must add though, you write rather well for your age. "Russet evenings" and "crimson mornings"! You seem to adore Annaville and I am glad you enjoy it. By the way, I remember, your birthday is only a few weeks away. Happy birthday!'

This was a Samir I had almost lost to years of cold silence and angry sarcasm so, enthused by his unspoken eagerness to start some kind of a dialogue, I wrote my first letter to him and then could not stop. I wrote to him furiously at night and cleared paper avalanches from my floor in the morning. I sent the sheets to him only after double-checking all the spellings. When I saw the way he folded his letters, I began to crisply crease mine the same way as well.

Whenever I heard a soft thump in the letter-box, scabs of reserve fell from an open wound that began once again to smart with love.

I wrote to him about the classes I would take in college. My longing for college lawns, canteen samosas and a grown-up library smelling of old wood, musty books and new magazines.

He wrote about his badminton tournaments. His experiments in the kitchen. The pine-apple wine he had made recently. His dreams of studying abroad. I often closed my eyes and saw him lounging on a planter's chair in Annaville's veranda. In a menthol-white shirt and faded khaki trousers.

He became the boy in the Tripp commercial, smiling at a young girl across the revolving door of a restaurant. I was the girl he was smiling at and then we were at the restaurant table, sipping the fuzzy, fizzy lemon drink from the same bottle. Whenever my letters grew too long, he grew quiet. Then, coming back from school, I would suddenly find a letter from him again with an urgent 'I do wait for your letters and count on you to be regular even when I can't write that often. Do write back soon'.

I emptied a large chocolate box of my trinkets and placed each of Samir's letters between folds of faded gift wrappers. The box became an affront to the world that had denied him to me. I began to believe in the miraculous power of chocolate boxes full of unconfessed love. Mine would claim Samir from the rest of the world, from the girl smelling of lime blossoms, from the scented letters and embroidered greeting cards he got in his mail from girls in his college.

In the same week I joined a women's college, Papu got a new job in Noida, a few hours away from us in Patiala. He returned every weekend with a briefcase crammed with dresses and plastic earrings for me and imported chocolates for Ma.

Punjab, however, was still choking on gun-powder. Every time Papu went to Noida in a morning bus, we worried if he would be marked by invisible terrorists, asked his Hindu name, pushed out of the bus and shot dead. He often talked to me about Bhinderwale, the blue ghost with the long flowing beard who was trying to convince both Hindus and Sikhs that they did not belong together. He headed an army of terrorists who bit into cyanide capsules when they were caught, hid amidst sugarcane clumps when they were cornered and fired bullets on bus passengers when no one was watching except their victims.

'You know the irony of it?' he asked me once, forking a masala-coated soya nugget that Ma had served him with his Old Monk peg. 'The irony is that he is the creation of a political party and today he is no longer their genie. The bottle is broken. Now they are at his mercy. He wants to run his own government. But he and the politicians don't know one thing. Punjabis are not Hindus or Sikhs. They are Punjabis. You can kill them but not their love for their fields, their temples, their gurudwaras and each other. The Punjabis will beat back anyone who tries to rupture their Punjabiyat. This can't go on. The terrorists can only kill. How many will they kill? They will have to stop one day because their madness will not infect people like us. They will lose because, till today, no Sikh has killed a Hindu neighbour. No Hindu in Punjab thinks of the Golden Temple as the home of Bhinderwale. It is and will always remain a symbol of Punjabi faith.'

The day the Golden Temple was stormed by the army to flush out Bhinderwale, Papu was at home and glued to the television set. 'This,' he turned from the screen once to tell me, 'is madness.' He touched the kada that was as much a part of his wrist as skin and bone.

When the news of Bhinderwale's death was broken on television, Narain Singh, our old Sikh machine-man, came home. He had always looked as if he was dying of something, but now he looked more shrivelled than usual. His beard had turned white in a dry, brittle sort of a way. As if it had been starched stiff and was crying out for grease. The beard, his glazed gaze and stooping little shoulders were in mourning. His wife had recently committed suicide because of his debts and we knew that he was sometimes seen in the cremation ground at night, talking to her. Trying to explain something she had been in too much of a hurry to hear.

He sat on the edge of a sofa, clutching a glass of tea and warming his sad beard with it. He told Papu, 'The government is lying Captain saab. Bhinderwale cannot die. I saw him at the cremation ground. He was alive. He told me he will address his people from Lahore TV. He had dug a tunnel under the Golden Temple which took him straight to Lahore. Pakistanis love Sikhs. They are taking good care of him.'

'Okay Narain, I believe you,' Papu said in a soft voice. 'He must be alive if you say so.'

'Yes, Captain saab!' Narain Singh's eyes began to blink

happily. 'He will address all Sikhs from Lahore TV at midnight.'

'Okay. Now go home and sleep if you have to be up at midnight,' Papu told him gently.

It wasn't long before India's prime minister was shot dead—and the mass killings of Sikhs began in Delhi. Kamalpreet Brar, my best friend in college, looked at me across the canteen table and told me her cousin, an NDA cadet, had been killed in Delhi. 'He was home for a few days and walking through a lonely short-cut after a late-night movie when they cornered him, put a tyre around his neck and set it on fire,' she told me, her eyes wider than usual. As if they were looking at something new. For some reason, I could not meet her eyes.

At home, we waited for word from Papu—Noida was not too far away from the lynching mobs. He came back after two weeks, looking pale. He was in Delhi when the riots broke out, he said. He did not tell us everything he'd seen but he seemed aware for the first time in his life that his Hindu home was just a wall away from houses thick with Sikhs.

He began to worry. 'I always believed men are not monsters. But maybe they are born monsters and only pretend to be human beings. I survived the riots because I wasn't a Sikh, but what if the Sikhs here decide to avenge those burnt on the streets of Delhi? What if they come knocking on our door? What if they find not me but just you both?'

Something hurtful and angry began to blow into our windows from Jattanwala Chauntra. Papu was cleaning the water tank on the terrace with Ma, when a teenaged Sikh boy, leaning down from an adjoining house, shouted, 'So Captain saab, Indira Gandhi died? No mourning ceremony in your house?'

Papu smiled and waved back, 'Kakaji, you don't know what I mourn for. But I am sure your father does. We played together as friends.'

Terrorism claimed a Sikh professor we were going to learn Shakespeare from. He had been married for not more than two months and was becoming known for his anti-militancy articles in newspapers. He was killed one evening while shopping for vegetables in a market.

A young police officer, a Sikh again, was shot dead when he was out jogging, a few blocks from his house.

The station director of All India Radio Patiala was kidnapped and found without his head in a ditch a few days later. He was a Hindu.

The newspapers told us that the terrorists no longer wanted to be called terrorists but militants. That young girls were now not to wear jeans. They had to wear white salwar kameez suits and cover their heads with saffron dupattas in college. That all clean-shaven Sikhs were now to grow beards and wear turbans. During our term exams, a few student leaders from a co-educational college stormed into our campus and sent our question papers flying out of the windows. But somehow Patiala's mohallas refused to jump into hate or fear.

*

A year before I was to graduate, Ma and I went to Noida to stay with Papu. He came in a Maruti van to pick us from

Delhi's Inter-State Bus Terminus. A driver opened the door for Ma and me to slide in. Ma looked out of the car window at something I could not yet see. She seemed afraid to smile and once touched Papu's tweed-clad arm to make sure that he was there next to the driver, looking back at her.

Delhi sprawled before us like a giant jigsaw puzzle. We craned our necks to look at the towering film hoardings. The endless rows of posters perched atop road dividers. The arrogant perfection of foreign embassies. The arched shadows of Connaught Place.

Delhi's shopping malls winked at me and jeered, 'You can't.'

But when I looked at Papu and then back at them, they grinned, 'Maybe you can.'

Delhi was a sea to Patiala's placid little lake. It had giant waves that everybody who came here had to learn to ride. It had cruel buses, peeling forts and cloud scrapers. It had a beggar who sat on a traffic junction, lost in his thoughts, forgetful of the reason why he was there. It had unending traffic. Rival newspapers waging battles on hoardings. Hot air balloons. Under bridges. Over bridges.

Papu's Noida flat was on the ground floor of a smart apartment building. It had a large bread box for a lawn in front and a kitchen garden in the backyard where the cook was growing red chillies that Papu loved and some cauliflowers. The walls were white, just like the house in Missamari, and Ma floated from room to room on a cloud.

The morning came smelling of Papu's aftershave lotion. I had not slept for half the night. I was afraid that if I closed my eyes, the world would dissolve, the house would vanish and I would wake up to see Ma and Papu sleeping on sand-dunes in a desert. Life was everything we had ever wanted it to be and maybe it was just a trick, just something beguiling before it was all taken away.

It was my birthday and Ma was already cooking in the kitchen. The cook was there too, diffidently holding out spices to her. After a lingering breakfast on a small dining table, Papu telephoned for the van again and we went to Delhi.

Papu was now a successful marketing manager and his company was making sure he did not stray. He got most of what he wanted now without overtly asking for it. He took us from one shop to another in the air-conditioned, colour-jammed corridors of Palika Bazaar. A faux snake-skin bag, Michael Jackson's *Thriller*, acid-washed jeans and a skirt with a slit at the back, a red, Wings t-shirt—he let me have it all.

He took us to a dim, cool restaurant and scolded Ma for reading out the price of each dish loudly. He took me to a stadium-sized bookshop and when I was walking out with a heap of fresh-smelling art books, he said, 'Now, don't ever make any excuses.'

But bound by our common fear of happiness, Ma and I sensed it was all too strange and new to be believed. We felt something lurking at our heels. We got home that evening and discovered a row of cars and white-washed faces in the building compound. A woman on the floor above us had died. Ma withered in her new, maroon silk saree.

Papu's faith in life was, however, being vindicated. He had paid off almost all his debts and won his mortgaged home back. He was becoming the success he was always meant to be. I looked at the harsh years of denial behind us but remembered no pain. I only remembered how he had celebrated them by dancing to a favourite song on the radio, by driving us on his scooter through rain all the way to Nahan, a leafy hill-town, for a picnic. Papu had no respect for tears. I remembered this when exactly four months after my memory-filled birthday, his colleague from Noida pressed our doorbell and told us that Papu had died of a massive heart-attack.

I stood straight and said in a voice that I hoped would reach Papu, wherever he was, 'Please come in and have a cup of tea.'

17

WE WENT TO Noida that night, Ma and I. From the taxi, Ma looked at the lights streaming past us and asked, 'What will we do?'

I smiled and told her with the confidence of someone who could not fail, 'Live.'

We went to the hospital to bring him to his home. I let nothing hurt me. Not even the small tufts of cotton that I was given to plug his nostrils and to soak the oozing gray liquid of death. Even when I saw him being wheeled out from the morgue on a stretcher, I did not acknowledge willingly that Papu had finally given in to a force bigger than him. He looked gray and his small mouth was that of a new-born baby in deep sleep after an exhausting struggle for life. He looked alone, vanquished. Dead down to the roots of his beautiful, salt-and-pepper hair.

His flat looked desolate. When Papu was eased onto a floor mattress in the drawing room, to rest and wait for his final journey to the cremation ground, the cook came to stand next to him, not knowing what to do. Slowly the mourners began to file in. When I went into Papu's bright bathroom to wash myself, I began to sing. *'Seene main jalan, ankhon mein toofan sa kyon hai, is shehar mein har shaks, pareshan sa kyon hai . . .'* I sang loudly. Papu loved my voice. I wanted him to hear it.

At the cremation ground, smoke watered my dry eyes as I watched Papu's hair curling in the crackling fire. I stood erect as if waiting for a cue before an audition. I was aware of nothing but my posture and the way my arm encircled Ma's tight, frozen shoulders. The way Papu's oversized blue jacket engulfed my slender body and how Ma's altered red bell-bottoms (with the bells taken off) felt on my legs.

I watched the burning wood and melting flesh that, not so long ago, was vibrant and living and had anchored us to life. But I felt no grief even when I picked up the Sikh kada he had worn all his life on his wrist, from the cinders. Papu's faith had outlasted him.

Later in the evening, when I spoke to Ma about the imperishability of life despite death, someone coughed loudly to shut me up. I knew, even if no one else did, that I had to live up to the responsibility of a life without Papu. I was playing to an invisible gallery suspended from the inky-blue night sky filled with Papu's applause.

I was not conscious of anything except that Ma had been grievously hurt again by life and that I was suddenly a word processor and a mind-reader with an X-ray vision. I could see through people now as if they were made of glass. I heard not just what was said but what was implied.

I began to see that Papu had finally caved in not only to death but also to people who would now walk into what was his kingdom and soil it with their dirty, hungry, curious shoes. Ma's father had lost his world in a more brutal way, but I felt the same anger Ma must have felt when a mob was dismantling her parents and their life.

I heard a whisper, 'Naaaice flat. Never knew he could afford a place like this.' It had escaped from Nimmo aunty. While she fussed over Ma and me, her eyes wandered all over the house. She scooted to the toilet to relieve her notoriously leaky bladder and came out looking disoriented. Her eyes were like a pair of restless bees, forming arches of motion above a cluster of flowers. She squirmed and then burst out, 'I wonder where he got the shower curtain from . . .' She trailed off, looking hopefully at me.

The mob had moved in, not with swords and knives, but with hurriedly-stuffed bags. Their clothes smelt not of blood but of overnight buses. Their eyes wandered too. To the shining kitchen top. To the carefully-tended pots that lined the small patch of green outside the house. To the pastel curtains that both Ma and Papu had selected during their last holiday together.

Naren uncle was heard complaining loudly about the food and insisted he be served spinach rice in the night. With baby potatoes coated in cumin seeds and home-ground spices. He also spent a lot of time telling the priests not to involve me in any rituals since daughters could not be forgiven for not being sons.

'Papu did not like any rituals so there won't be any. The priests can leave. And no, Ma will not wear white or sit with any of these women who have been wailing loudly since morning,' I told him as his eyes and nose grew bigger with indignation.

There was also a man I never saw again, who stood

admiring himself in the mirror of Papu's dressing table. He gingerly touched his eau de cologne bottle, and then in a sudden spurt of bravado, sprayed it all over himself. I took the bottle and hid it in Ma's suitcase.

Anna aunty was holidaying in Europe with her family and couldn't be reached, but Manna aunty came with Anu and immediately monopolised the best pillows in the house. She specified the size of the butter dollop that was to be served with Anu's rotis. She looked disgruntled at the sight of the flowers blooming in their little bed in the lawn. But was reassured to see Ma's crumpled figure. Ma had never been expected to amount to anything, and she had placated Manna aunty by getting widowed early in life.

I told Ma that I would start looking for a job and she smiled with pride and looked at the circle of relatives around her, 'Look at her! As if she needs to worry about all this!'

Then we got ready to come back to Patiala with a truck packed with Papu's short-lived success. I still felt unscathed and nothing could yet touch me. Not the fundamental vocabulary of death at least. It was life and the smallest of things in it that hurt. Like the oblivious, radiant windows that glowed from warm, happy homes.

Ma made another departure from hope. This time with sorry little potted plants from Papu's lawn, his suitcases and the casseroles that she had arranged on his beautiful kitchen shelves. We left on a bleak afternoon, without a backward glance at the cheerful cauliflowers and chillies Papu had grown in the backyard. We left, trying not to look back at the slanting shadows and swatches of sunlight still snuggling the walls of Papu's empty flat.

18

WE WENT BACK to a house that had just been beginning to look prosperous. Ma's arms were bare now. The wings had disappeared. She did not know what to do without a husband whose needs had defined her life. Now that she was not to switch on the geyser in preparation for his weekend visits, not cook soya chunks with his favourite masala, not sip beer from his glass, not unpack his suitcase and not see him off on Monday mornings, she did not know what to find joy in.

Ma had longed for Anna aunty all through but after her holiday, she was now in the US to finalise a hotel management course for Samir. I waited to hear from Samir, but it was almost as if our letters to each other had been written in a time zone that no longer existed.

It was almost one year before Anna aunty could come to us. She entered our home with a large suitcase on wheels, filled with happy fabrics and pretty mementos. She smelt of new places and looked at us with wide, dark eyes that had never mourned an irretrievable slice of life. She made me want to scream out in agony.

But it was when she placed her jar of cocoa butter cream and a long necked, slim-waisted perfume bottle on Ma's forlorn dressing table that I really mourned the death of happiness in our life. When she ran her hands down the crisp folds of her saree and looked at herself in the mirror, I ached for everything that had gone out of Ma's life with Papu. Her joy in her femininty and his presence. The immediacy of touch and warmth, laughter and love.

Once reassured that my education was in no danger of being interrupted because we had Papu's pension and my scholarship, Anna aunty nodded, packed our suitcases and took us to Ambrosa. Samir was back for a brief vacation, but the house told me he wasn't inside. The prospect of him staying away from Annaville for a few years did not unsettle me. I knew he would never think any woman important enough to alter the course of his future. I climbed up on to my window seat and was trying to read a news magazine with a full-lipped, feathered Pamela Bordes on the cover when I heard his footsteps.

'Where is she?' I heard him ask impatiently, and in a moment saw his tall shadow framed by the door. I knew then without a shadow of doubt, that he had waited for me through long winter days, opened my letters in the darkness of his room and read them in the pool of light under his study lamp and agonised over the difference between 'with love' and 'lots of love' at the end of each.

A moment passed and then he slowly walked towards me. He smiled as if he did not know that he was smiling and then stopped, opened his arms and whispered, 'Darling'. The blood froze in my heels. And the faded wooden floor throbbed, waiting to sear me from end to end. I got up, faced him and said, 'Hi!'

It sounded wrong. The 'i' did not end properly. It should have embraced him. Instead, it fell on a cold snatch of the floor between him and me. I saw a pair of nutmeg-speckled eyes grow dark. I heard a door being shut even before it was closed.

I walked past Samir's closed door, torn between fear and sliced in two halves by the pain of making him leave the room empty-handed. When the pain became too much and Ma asked, 'Why are you gritting your teeth?', I knocked on Samir's door. He took his time to open it. When he finally did, he leaned against it quietly, and watched me struggle with words. 'I just wanted to . . . can you show me around? Or just take me for a ride?'

'Okay,' he said, without any anger or warmth, put on his denim jacket and took a bunch of keys from the table. He walked out of the house without looking back. His motorcycle was roaring before I could shut the door behind me. I sat behind him, clutching the back rest, both feet on one side. When he was riding past the tea-gardens, I spoke to him. 'You know . . .' I grew reckless and added despite the fear that gnawed at my gut, 'I was so scared.'

He slowed down, turned around to look at me and said, 'Why? Are you scared of me?'

The afternoon was golden and it would have been so easy to rest my face against his warm, denim jacket and run my fingers through his hair, feel the nape of his neck and clasp him in my arms. It would have been so easy for him to stop, take me to the edge of a mountain, hold me close against himself. And then perhaps push me off the cliff.

I didn't touch him. But clenched my fear between my teeth and whispered, 'I was scared you would not bring me along, that you would leave me behind.'

'Why would I do something like that? To you of all people?' he said softly and added, 'As if . . .'

When he stopped at a petrol station, we could not look at each other. The attendant smiled at him and looked at me with unabashed curiosity. Next we stopped at the grocer's and Samir bought some pasta and cheese. We rode back home in complete silence, but I caught a glimpse of his profile. It was edged with sunlight and a smile. He took the longest route to Annaville and we reached home to find Anu waiting for us. It was a flying visit, she chirped, and disappeared in Samir's arms. The evening slipped away from us.

After dinner, we threw a rug on the veranda and sat together to watch the stars. Samir lay sprawled across the rug, his eyes closed. He propped himself against an elbow, and said to me drowsily, 'Sing us something.'

I sang a song I'd heard him listening to earlier in the day, '*Koi ye kaise bataye ke woh tanha kyon hai . . .*'

Even when I grew quiet, Samir did not open his eyes. He hummed, '*Jhuki jhuki si nazar bekraar hai ki nahin . . . daba daba sa sahi dil main pyar hai ki nahin.*'

Anu burst out laughing, 'Hush. Don't let the cook hear you. He will lose all respect and never serve you your waffles on time.'

Samir looked at me and said in a quiet voice, 'You know Anu, you should read the letters she writes to me.'

Anu stopped laughing and looked at him.

Then she looked at me and began to laugh again. 'I don't believe this,' she gasped between hiccups.

Samir clasped his hand over her mouth and said, 'Both of us love Jagjit Singh and Kaifi Azmi. She is a bright little girl and I enjoy her letters. What's so funny about that?'

Anu was looking intently at him and he noticed that.

When he spoke again, his tone was half-jocular. The kind he adopted always to speak to me in company.

'You know, I was so eager to meet this girl and guess how she greeted me? She looked up from a magazine, said "Hi", and went back to it again!'

I was livid and snapped back, 'What do you think I should have done? Should I have . . .'

I could not complete the sentence, could not meet either his or Anu's eyes. When I looked up he was smiling and his eyes lingered for just a moment on my mouth before he got up and said, 'Anyway, there is always a next time. Come on girls. It is very late and I have to get back to my books.'

19

I FELL ASLEEP, listening to the faint hum of Jagjit Singh in his room. I was growing one year older the next day and I could not wait for dawn. The room was full of Ambrosa's morning mist when I woke up. A lone bird sang outside the window. Ma was asleep. So was the rest of the house. The window opposite the bed was a shade of pale bougainvillea pink. I watched it for some time and then turned over to sleep again when something grazed my cheek. A small packet reposed next to my pillow. Pinned on it was a greeting card carrying messages from everyone in Annaville.

The packet was gift-wrapped in gold roses. I opened the packet cautiously, taking care not to tear the precious paper. A gold rimmed diary lay inside. Its milky-white core encased in mocha leather. On the first page was written, 'For the days when you may not have anyone to write to! Love, Samir'.

Love, Samir. Love, Samir.

He had never used that word before.

I had barely finished re-reading the message when I heard

Samir's motorbike purring away. 'Some errand,' Anna aunty told me as she kissed me happy birthday over the breakfast table. Anu made a long shopping list between mouthfuls and began to coax Anna aunty and Ma to take her to the market. I excused myself and disappeared for a long bath with Anna aunty's birthday gifts. A cocoa butter shower cream, a green apple shampoo and bath salts in long bottles.

When I came out smelling confusedly of lavender and cocoa butter, the house was quiet. I walked through the long corridors towards the stairs to get to the terrace. The rooms on the first floor were hardly used except when a large number of people gathered at the house. They held no charm for me. I had no memories of them. The terrace had many. Stone benches I had sat on with Samir's comics, an old hammock from Samir's room, sunshine and silence. I shut the terrace door behind me, removed the towel wrapped around my hair and raised my face to the sun. The hammock moved suddenly and I saw Samir raising his head to look at me.

I swung towards the door in mindless panic. 'Where are you running away?' I heard him ask. I turned around. He moved to stand against the parapet, his hands planted behind him and legs crossed.

I smiled back weakly, 'Sorry, I didn't mean to disturb you.'

'First things first. Happy birthday. And the second thing. I am standing very far from you. I'll stay here, I promise. Don't be scared.'

I could see nothing, feel nothing, except his eyes. I snapped, 'I am not scared of you.'

'Then sit down,' he said, and pointed to a bench.

I sat down. On the floor was a tray with two glasses of orange juice in it.

'I know you come here to dry your hair,' he explained. 'Drink it up.'

I picked up the glass and gave him his when he walked up to me. He sat down on a chair opposite me and began to look at a point just above my head.

'So, what do you intend doing after you graduate?' he asked.

'I don't know,' I said.

'Seriously?'

'Seriously,' I nodded.

'Do you want something, anything from life?' he asked.

'Happiness,' I gulped

His eyes rested on me. 'And how do you intend to find it?'

'It will come.'

He shook his head, 'How do you know it won't move on? If you want something, never wait for it to come to you—that's something I live by.'

I could feel his eyes searching my face for something, but I didn't look up. I stayed impassive and drank in the glow of his presence, not letting him know how every word he spoke burnt itself into my memory and stayed there forever.

'I want happiness too, but I already have so much of it. And have no patience with what cannot be mine. I am never at the mercy of life. You shouldn't be either,' he said.

He put his glass down and leaned forward. 'Do you know how lovely you look when you smile? What stops you from doing that more often? From talking to me? From cracking a casual joke? When you write those letters, I can see right through you. When I meet you, I only see a frowning wall. What is it that splits you up like this? Why do you run away from everything that you want? Why don't you take what is yours?'

My face was burning by now and my courage was a knot in my throat.

But I still managed to say, 'Why don't you, Samir?'

I closed my eyes and waited for him to walk up to me and burn us both alive. The world grew quiet and I heard it only when Samir shut the terrace door behind him and was gone.

When I came down, he was stretched on a carpet in the drawing room, laughing over some masks that Anu had brought from the market. There was no disquiet on his face. I stumbled over a Tibetan bell and Anu caught me just before I fell down. 'Handle her with care Anu,' he said. I sat down next to him and smiled at him. He smiled back.

Anu was still the glossy, statuesque girl who had once found me alternately abhorrent and pitiable but we were equals now and she recognised this immediately. And not just because I had more poise now than when she had first seen me at Annaville.

I was no longer apologetic or afraid of being hurt by either of them and Samir was no longer the centre of her existence. Though she looked guilelessly surprised everytime Samir humoured or placated me, she was unaffected by his attention to me.

'I am seeing somebody,' she smiled broadly at Samir.

He shook his head, 'You? You can actually "see" somebody beyond yourself? Wonderful!'

'Shut up you ass,' she hollered, 'shut up . . . he's . . .' and then, 'I am having a lot of problems because Mummy is going ballistic. She thinks I can do better because he is not the "right stock".'

Samir immediately sobered up, 'Just do what you want. It is the hardest and the simplest thing to do. And if you need any help in transporting Manna aunty somewhere no one can find her, just say the word.'

In the evening, Anu and he decided to cook pasta for me and sat me down on a low cane stool in the kitchen to 'observe and learn'. Anu blanched tomatoes and squished them in the blender and Samir chopped green peppers in thin slivers and often smiled for no reason. There was a roar outside. 'It's going to rain,' Anu looked at the blue windows. Samir opened the door that led to the kitchen garden and let the rain-cooled wind in through the meshed screen. Soon the only light in the kitchen was rose and amber and it came from the swaying stained glass lamps that Anna aunty had suspended from a beam across the ceiling.

Anu continued talking about her love life, 'It was so sudden for me . . . like he was a stranger one minute and then in the next, boom, *there* he was. We were in a canteen and he was with another boy I was talking to. He did not say much but, I don't know why, throughout the conversation, I grew more and more conscious of him. I saw him run his hands through his hair and I don't know why, the way he did it . . . stayed with me. I dreamt that night that he was with me in my room and his face was a breath away . . . and the way he was looking at me. God! You know, I don't fall to pieces easily, but just the sight of him in the canteen, the next day! The first two buttons of his shirt were open and don't laugh, I actually began to picture in my head what his chest hair would look like!'

Samir turned to look at me and said, 'Well, of course you did Anu. So did it go any further? I mean, did you actually see his chest hair?'

Anu punched him and shook her head. 'No, but I intend to!'

I suddenly wanted to escape and got up, 'I'm feeling a bit cold here so can I leave please? I'm not hungry anyway.'

I willed Samir to look up from the pan where a fiery sauce bubbled, and when he did, his mouth was full with a smile.

'Stay or I will find you wherever you are and probably stuff your face with my bare hands,' he said.

'I won't eat your hands either,' I said defiantly, and he threw his head back and laughed.

'Now you know, Anu, why I'm crazy about her.'

Anu just smiled. She was busy tossing the pasta in the sauce. Then she looked at the white sheath trembling on the window. 'Joker. He says, he's crazy about every second girl he meets but I must tell you this,' she looked at me, 'there was one time when I actually believed him. Samir and I were watching the rain from the veranda once and he said the rain reminded him of her. You know about her?'

I met her eyes squarely. 'No,' I said.

Samir was washing his hands in the sink. He did not say anything.

'He had met this girl in Jaipur on a holiday. He told me later she was the only girl he felt totally, helplessly in love with. I have seen her pictures. Short, small, a boyish mop. I could not see her eyes. She wore dark shades in all the pictures. She looked like a dairy-fresh vanilla scoop. Not the kind he usually falls for.'

'And what kind is that?' I asked evenly.

She lifted one brow and grimaced, 'You know, long legs, great breasts ... Oh, don't blush now! I'm sure you're old enough to know that most boys notice your body first and what's inside later. But this girl, apparently, was different. She was innocent and she did not notice him noticing her. So she did not respond at all and, understandably, he was a goner—totally destroyed. Sex is not big deal for him. There, I have said the word, now stop looking as if I have defecated on Anna aunty's dining table! Sex comes easy to him. It's love that is hard for him. And the only girl who will ever get to him is the one he cannot get. He just could not stop talking about her. He grew his beard. He even went on a drinking binge till Inder uncle pulled him up!'

When she finished, she looked for a long moment at me. I stared back evenly, not letting her see if her words had made any mark. Not knowing if she had been trying to test my composure or if it was just an innocent, well-meaning remark. Or if she was warning me.

She left the next morning. I had nothing to say to Samir through the day. I sat alone in the veranda, looking at the garden, waiting for the moment it would lose its glow and grow dark, when Samir appeared by my side like a golden apparition. He had a sheaf of photographs in his hands. 'Here ... some pictures clicked with friends.'

I began to look at them one by one. I saw her photograph too. Dressed in a pink, embroidered top, dark blue jeans, photographed in the last glimmer of a Jaipur sunset.

'Her name is Preeti and I really liked her because she just

seemed so uncomplicated and everytime I met her, I was someone different ... from the person I am. I realise now that it was not real because she did not really know who I was. She was just a simple, straightforward girl who would have been happy with another simple, straightforward guy. There have been others ... like this girl I dated for a while who said she could not go out with me anymore because I was probably only going to end up trapped in my father's life in Ambrosa! It was hilarious that she believed we were actually headed towards a future! No one knows what I feel or how much about anyone or anything.'

He waited for me to say something and then said, 'Anu is my buddy and she is right. Sex is a simple thing for me. I understand passion. I don't know that much about love. But if two people have passion, it should be enough, no?'

I said, trying to find the words to say something that I knew he was not capable of understanding now, 'Passion without love, I don't understand. I ... I am just not like that. It would destroy me to give myself to someone who did not love me.'

I went to the next picture where Samir was under a waterfall, stripped to the waist. He took the picture from me.

'This was taken at Jog Falls during a college trip to Shimoga. I wish the place were close by. I would have taken you there and dunked you in the waters.' I looked at him. His eyelids were heavy, fevered. He began to laugh. 'The only problem is, you probably would have died of pneumonia! You have nothing on your bones.'

'I have a lot up here,' I tapped my head and snapped.

'And little good it has done you,' he grinned and added,

'Maybe what you have up there is part of the problem.'

Anna aunty came out with a watering can and smiled at me. 'Why do you always look so crushed? You are so pretty ... so bright,' she said to me as she drenched a rose bush from leaf to leaf.

I smiled at her, 'Nothing can crush me. If Papu's death could not do it, I don't see how anyone or anything can. If I can live without him, I can live without anyone. But the thing is, Papu spoilt me because he taught me to want everything from life as if I deserve nothing less. It is just that, if I am offered less, I don't want it. I want it all or nothing.'

Samir took the album from me and snapped, 'Oh, so that's what it is? You can live without anything or anyone? Really, are you sure about that? I hope you don't ever have to find out the real meaning of what you just said. And you make life and death decisions by overhearing conversations between other people? By listening hard to things and people you shouldn't? She's going to be a lot of trouble Ma ... to herself and to some poor sod who falls for her. Just look at her and look at that frown—trouble all over.'

Anna aunty looked at me and then at him, her face conflicted between confusion and exhaustion and I got up to leave.

I heard him saying to my back with a loud, dramatic sigh. 'Back to square one ... back to square one.'

Later that evening, while looking for a ball of twine for Anna aunty in the store room, I burst into tears. I had not really cried for Papu because I had never really felt his absence to a point where tears were necessary to mourn him. I still felt that tears were not the appropriate response to his life because all the years he was alive were more important than his death but the tears would not stop.

I heard Samir before I saw him. 'Why are you crying?' his voice was almost tender.

He caught me by my shoulders and peered down at me, 'Did I say something . . . back there in the veranda that . . .?

I shook my head.

Face-to-face with something he had never come up against, he muttered ineffectually, 'Come on now. Okay? You're missing your dad?'

I nodded.

He let go of me, 'You've been so mature about this whole thing. I know, believe me I know, just how strong you are, so no more tears, okay?'

'Why did you never write to me—after Papu?' I asked, wiping my tears.

He looked sheepish and played with the edge of a rusty knife absently, 'I didn't know what to write. I am not good with this stuff. I knew you would manage and come through and I can see, you have.'

In the days that followed, he became gentler, and more patient with me. He sat with me and leafed though my books, pored over my sketches, smiled at the nudes I had copied from my art books. He said, 'This is passion. So this is where you spend it, hmm? I can see the future, right here. One day you will have an exhibition of paintings and I will be at the door of the gallery, ushering visitors!'

The night before Ma and I were to leave for Patiala, he took me for a stroll through the garden and I sensed an unease in his limbs as he walked next to me. The sidewalks were thick with tuberoses and their fragrance imbued every thing, even the stars, and I felt I could pluck them all from the sky and smell each one.

Samir's eyes were downcast, intent on the darkness spread beneath his feet. He was weighing something and I suddenly felt the urge to talk without any reason because I knew a long silence would plunge us both in a frightful awareness of each other. And then something molten and livid and hungry would take us over.

The moment passed almost as soon as it came and he quietly took out a cigarette from his pocket and began to smoke. 'You are leaving tomorrow?' he asked.

I nodded.

He was quiet for a moment and then said, 'I am not a romantic. I don't dream or imagine things that are not there. I understand real things. I told you that I understand passion and I know that nothing compares to it, nothing. I know more about these things than you do and I know that passion does not last. But as long as it stays, you really don't need anything else from life. Don't be mad when I say this, but most women don't want to admit it. They want something beyond passion and not many men know what that is.'

He had said all that he had wanted to, but the block of black ice that always jutted between us remained undissolved.

I asked, 'So how many times has this . . . passion . . . come and gone?'

He laughed, 'If I told you, you would run away. You don't have a great opinion about me anyway, do you?'

'Samir, what do you want from me?'

'Nothing,' he suddenly threw his cigarette down and crushed it with the tip of his shoe. He said, 'You know, when I was small, I thought that the sky was a giant dartboard. I still think that in a way. I have always had what I wanted but . . . . .' Then he turned and looked at me and we walked back to the house, unresolved and in silence.

Next morning, when Anna aunty was mixing some sprouts with chopped onions for our train tiffin, Samir appeared, looking a bit dishevelled. He was in his vest and blue, drawstring trousers. There was a faint stubble on his jaw. 'Go and shave Mir,' she smeared his cheek with a little tomato juice.

'Problem Ma . . . my whole life is nothing but darkness and I can't shave in the dark,' he said, wrapping his arms around her.

'Get lost,' she laughed and shooed him out with a wooden ladle.

She looked at me. 'You are laughing,' she smiled and then grew sombre. 'There was this girl he had met in Jaipur just before we left for Europe and he kept corresponding with her all through last year. Her family wanted a certain kind of boy for her and Samir frightened them because he does not care about feigning politeness when he does not feel any. He spoke once or twice to her parents but said nothing that could reassure them. They found an IAS officer for her and the girl got engaged recently. He is hurting, but he will get over it.'

I grew cold. And the visit ended with long uninterrupted nothingness between us.

20

AFTER WE GOT back, Samir's letters came in a trickle between long droughts.

For weeks, I dreamt of a giant banyan tree with dense matted darkness and lit a lamp under its dreadlocks. The lamp would burn for a while and then give up. One night, as I was trying to relight the lamp, the doorbell rang and woke me up.

I padded to the bedroom window to see who or what was at the door. Ma came out of the sliding door of her bedroom and together we looked down into the street. In the green-blue circle of the street-light, we saw a man. Pressing the bell and looking up at us. The moment he saw our faces, he bared his teeth like shining white weapons. He took out a slim, square packet from his pocket and lifted it up under the light for us to see. It had the picture of a naked woman with abnormally large breasts. In the unreal light, they looked like two, large, dim bulbs. He slipped the packet in the tin letterbox and took his finger off the bell. He was about to reach for his crotch, when Ma pulled me back and drew the curtain tight. Before she could say anything, I tore the curtains apart and screamed at him, 'Hey, don't entertain us alone. Let me call the whole mohalla and then we will all sit in a circle and see your thing.' A door opened somewhere and startled the man. He zipped up his trouser, spat at the window and bounded into the night.

In the morning, Ma cleared the letter-box of the condom packet. A few days later, when I was coming back from college, I heard some footsteps behind me. I began to run. I did not need to look behind to know that hormones are neither Hindu nor Sikh. They erupted with the same demonic perversity in all groins and all faces.

When I could not run any more, the boys caught up. I froze, trying to flatten my body against a wall when a boy walked close to me, reached out and grabbed my breast. The world emptied itself except for my breast and the hand on it. I rammed my head into the boy's chest and my knee jammed his crotch against his buttocks. 'Saali!' he screamed and the boys who had been standing and watching my breast with his hand on it, took to their heels. I ran after them. I saw their legs, running in blurred circles towards a manhood they had not yet reached.

When I could see nothing but a little empty square made up of doors they had shut themselves in, I stood and screamed, 'Come out . . . try your luck one more time.'

I was growing taller than Bakshi Ganda Singh Street. My outbursts of rage were debilitating and sudden and they exploded against large men who brushed their elbows against my hips in the bazaars or commented on the zippers of the acid-washed jeans that Papu had bought for me. I felt violated by an ignorant, malfunctioning world and men who leered regardless of grief walking inside nubile bodies.

When I walked past shops lined with high-heeled, broad-toed, silk-tasselled, bead-encrusted mojris, I realised that, without Papu, I could no longer look at the gifts of life with a sense of ownership. Ma's deep-rooted darkness that had lightened in the last triumphant sun-burst in Papu's life, was beginning to grow vengefully strong inside me.

I yearned for cups of evening coffee in Anna aunty's veranda. I missed Anna aunty in a pashmina shawl, eating ginger biscuits with Samir and recollecting with laughter, how ET got drunk on a can of beer. I remembered all the gifts she had given me. Hand-knitted, woollen ponchos, long skirts, sweaters, affection and a diffident hope that life could be willed to be beautiful. And I knew there was one gift I would never get from her. Samir would never be mine and I forgot this only when I painted, perched on a stool in the college studio. I painted the cool, shady patches of the college property. I saw no one. Not the girls on scattered stools. Not the disapproving teacher who told me that my landscapes were too green for the Indian summer. 'Our trees are dusty green. Not monsoon fresh. You will never be able to paint realistically.'

Then Ma received a letter from Mandi. Anu had eloped and gotten married to Vikram. The same boy who, according to Manna aunty, was beneath her. We took a bus to Mandi and carried our best wishes to the well-furnished house where Anu had been brought up. She was home to get 'accepted' formally.

I saw her taking long strolls in the garden with her husband. Vikram was not strikingly handsome, but I immediately saw how someone as self-assured as Anu had found him irresistible. He was playful with her, attentive but not obsequious to either her or her parents. He had a presence that went beyond his deep-set eyes, the two undone buttons of his shirt and his easy smile.

I watched the way Anu followed him with her gaze and remembered with a pang Samir's infrequent and casual letters from an American college conveying excitement over the 'pretty scenery' everywhere.

I crouched under my quilt at night when Anu and Vikram shut the door of their room and played old Hindi film songs on an old tape-recorder. I wondered what it would be like to be alone with Samir in a home with white walls, blue curtains, low couches. On a cool, breezy moonlit night, Samir would stretch out on the balcony with a glass of wine. And I would walk around him. Kiss the back of his neck. Or the top of his head. Sip the wine from his mouth. Then we would sit quietly, cocooned in each other. My head would be against his chest.

In our house, there would be Ghalib's poetry. And Jagjit Singh. My Hindi films. His cowboy westerns. Cooking smells. Ceramic pottery. Fresh flowers. His books and mine in one bookshelf. His aftershave lotions and my perfumes in one drawer. Cupboards with his clothes and mine. There would be guests. And I would cook for them and he would grin with pride and pull me close to sit next to him. I would never wonder about love. Ghalib's sandstorms of hijr would give away to the blue oasis of visaal. From pining to consummation, we would come full circle. And talk a lot. Laugh a lot. Sometimes sulk. I would grow familiar with the smell of him. The feel of him. And the fine hair on the nape of his neck. I would know the taste of his mouth. I would never need to write letters to him. Never need to wait for him. Because he would never be far enough to be missed. He would not be a wrench, but an inner knowing. An invisible smile. A ring of joy around me.

Anu told me that Samir was in Ambrosa for a vacation. 'Anna aunty has house guests and can't come. Samir will. He can't wait to meet Vicky,' she trilled. I felt unhinged. I shivered under the quilt all night, my raw toes straining against sticky woollen socks. Even the quilt reeked of something wasting away inside me till a snatch of sunlight settled on the window pane and redeemed me.

Manna aunty was blundering into things and people like a frazzled rabbit and seemed ready to duck under a chair every time someone came in to congratulate the luminous couple.

Anu had been her pride and joy because her eyes laughed even when she did not and her lustrous hair reached her heels. She knew how to paint her lips perfectly with liquid lip colour. She knew how to make Russian salad and had topped her school. Her future had been sealed against any unforeseen circumstances by Manna aunty, but still there had been gaps through which she had escaped to find her own truth.

I remembered how, after Papu's funeral, Manna aunty had told Ma about her elaborate plans to marry Anu to an IAS officer, 'His parents live in a house with a porch and have a red car in the garage. But you don't worry, I will . . . we will do what we can for your girl.' I remembered her telling us when we were grieving, how prudent it would be to boil spent tea leaves again, reuse burnt matchsticks and buy second-hand books now that we could not afford a spanking new life. And now Anu had spoilt it all and married a medical student who hailed from a small village in Madhya Pradesh.

This was an unscheduled happening in Manna aunty's life and it had left her vulnerable before people like me whom she had dismissed with all the self-assurance that money and a green toilet seat in a freshly-renovated house could provide.

'Tell me honestly, what do you think about this? Would you marry someone like that just for love?' She was furiously rescuing overdone, plump pooris from the bubbling oil in the kadai and she sounded desperate. I felt stricken by her question, but told her what she needed to hear. Anu was still perfect and her life would always be envied, and she greedily drank in my disinterest in the bargain her daughter had struck with life. She piled the pooris in a thali and sashayed out to meet more guests, the old confidence almost back in her gait. Her genial husband smiled at me encouragingly, but I saw nothing except Anu and Vikram looking at each other over bobbing heads, sharing a blanket, laughing at jokes no one could understand, huddling together on a sunny sofa. And I ached for Samir and hovered around the window guiltily, famished for a glimpse.

21

I ALMOST DOUBLED up with pain when I saw him walking to the house with an overnight bag slung across his shoulders. He looked like the radiant windows I had been tortured by after Papu's death. Sheathed against mortality in his black sweater and an obviously new pair of jeans. It blurred the length of his legs. I did not like it. A new watch gleamed against his smooth, brown wrist.

I did not know what to do. So I crouched in the shadows and waited for him to claim me. A long time passed before he came to stand next to me. He enquired politely about my post-graduation plans and then, with a smile that filled me like warming wine, he said, 'You, are made for special things.'

He spent the rest of the day with Anu and Vikram, and occasionally his laughter wafted like a well-loved fragrance in the room where I sat with a book.

That night, after dinner, when he went to the terrace to steal a smoke, I followed him. He stood wreathed in smoke rings and smiled as if he were watching a prophecy being fulfilled.

A love song rasped on Anu and Vikram's new music system that Samir had gifted them. I felt like a fool on a railway track, about to enjoy the spectacle of his own mutilation. Goaded by a pain that could not be argued with, I spat out, 'What do I do?'

He smiled, 'With whom?'

'With you, of course,' I bristled.

He laughed, 'That you have to decide, you know. The prey never decides for the one who hunts.'

I interrupted him impatiently, 'Rubbish as usual, Samir! Who the hell is the prey here? Who is hunting whom? Can you ever come clean about what you really want me to do with this *thing* that is always between us? What did you say, it was? Short-lived passion? We have been dancing this dance since we were kids and you still think it is something to be trifled with? Do you even know what I am talking about?'

He stopped smiling.

His gaze, his jaw and voice were all stone-cold when he said, 'What *are* you talking about?'

I felt a sheet of ice pressing into my skin and my Tibetan sweater suddenly felt too thin for the Mandi cold.

'I love you,' I spat the words at him like a curse.

We both stood frozen for a second.

He moved first and then raised his hand as if to ward the words away, 'You're a nut.'

Then he lit another cigarette. It was a long moment because the cigarette was half gone when he spoke again, 'I'm in shock.' He shook his head and repeated, 'I'm in shock. That night in Annaville, when I spoke to you about passion, what made you think I was talking about us? I can't believe what happened in that awful farmhouse your dad took us to so many years ago is still such an issue for you that you have made it central to your existence. I have always wished you well because my mother adores you. To tell you the truth, I saw it coming. It's embarrassing, how you watch me with those droopy eyes of yours. But you'll outgrow it. A couple of my juniors in New Jersey are keen to marry Indian girls. Financial status no bar. I was thinking of talking to your mother about them. I can also help you with money. But this is really . . .'

He was still talking when I left the terrace. I was wading through the darkness of the guest room to get to my bed when Ma turned in her bed and whispered, 'Where were you? Don't tell me you are going to sleep in your jeans. Your pyjamas are on the chair. Go change.'

I didn't and just shook my shoes off before crawling under the warmth of my quilt. I shivered like an animal slowly dying under a cold, night sky and stayed awake all night. I knew exactly when Samir came to shave in the bathroom next to our room. I heard him brush his teeth. Heard splashes of water. When I came out of the room, he was already at the table, eating the pancakes Anu had made for him . He didn't look up from his plate and I walked past him to the kitchen to join Anu.

A few minutes later Samir shook off the crumbs of last night from his memory and was ready to go. He hugged Anu and nodded at me when a taxi drove up at the gate to take him to Ambrosa. When I saw Samir's taxi zoom towards his gold and white world, I hugged myself, trying to shield something that had been cut open without an anaesthetic.

A few weeks later, I bled for the last time. Anna aunty had come down to Patiala to spend a week with us. On the morning she was to leave, we walked her to the mouth of Sarhindi Bazaar through the shivering silence. We walked past the half-hearted growls of a few sleepy dogs. 'Never wake the sleeping dogs in Bakshi Ganda Singh Street,' Anna aunty chuckled. An icy wind flapped my umbrella sleeves against my thin wrists when I pulled Anna aunty's bag over the jagged, cruel street.

'Be careful, the wheels are rusty,' Ma said once.

When a rickshaw grated to a halt next to us, Anna aunty turned to us and said, 'Oh yes, I forgot to tell you . . . Samir has decided to work for good in the US. In a few months from now, he will be managing a resort in Vegas.'

She sounded happy, proud and forlorn, 'He won't come back. I just know he won't. He is very happy though.'

She hugged us both and then got into the rickshaw. I put her bag next to her and she was gone. We walked back home. It was in the light of the drawing room that I noticed. My left foot was covered with blood. Ma let out a little cry, 'That wheel! I told you to be careful.'

Ma bathed my foot with Savlon and warm water, bandaged it and went to sleep. I slowly sat down on the sofa. I felt my insides heaving. I cried till I was empty. In the days that followed, I felt nothing. When I looked into the mirror, I saw nothing. One morning, I went to call Anna aunty from an STD booth. I got Samir's address from her and sat up late into the night writing to him.

I promised myself it would be the last time. I remembered the morning in Samir's garden when I had sat under an arch of blossoms, feeling blessed. I had to give myself one more chance to find out if that moment had any meaning. I stopped when the day broke over my head. I posted the letter and never heard from him again. When a New Year card addressed to Ma arrived from the US with a photograph of Samir at his hotel's bar-counter, flashing a smile under a newly-sprouted moustache, I felt liberated. It was the moustache. It did not look that good. Did he think he could get away with everything? The chocolate box was empty now. The years he had spent writing to me had disappeared. Anna aunty wanted me to come and visit her before my graduation. But before I could decide whether to go to her or not, the floods came.

22

PATIALA'S RESIDENT RIVER broke its parched banks to storm into the city. It swelled and raged, swallowed electric poles, fields and the somnolent life in the areas skirting the town. It rushed headlong into homes and broke doors and hearts and turned dreams into mud. The floods coaxed snakes nestling in the town's muddy underbelly, to swim out in shivering streaks of motion. When the river showed no sign of abating, the army was called in. Helpless refrigerators and bodies floated past soldiers in rescue boats.

Families crouched on roofs and treetops. The edges of the town got submerged but the naturally-elevated walled city and its mohallas, one of which was ours, stayed dry. The flood, in a hurry to destroy everything in its way, passed us by to attack low-lying areas. There was no electricity in the town. The windows stayed dark through dull days and lamp-lit nights. The air stank of rotting wheat kernels in the grain market, disintegrating fruit in locked shops, soggy garbage and rain trapped within walls.

I went to the terrace sometimes and saw an occasional helicopter whirring overhead. I heard shouts of glee as the neighbourhood children jumped high and waved their hands to the invisible pilot and minister surveying the town. On a slightly bright day, Ma and I went to see the rest of the city. The heart of the town looked mangled. Quila Chowk had been turned into a refugee camp. The Shiva temple was hemmed in by limp tents. Trucks packed with large pots of khichdi and boxes full of old clothes from distant villages crowded the town square. Robust Sikhs and Hindu volunteers stirred food in cauldrons and fed the hungry.

The flood had washed away the remaining dregs of mistrust. The two communities were back to being inseparable like a nail is from the skin surrounding it. Ma and I joined the chain of volunteers and served food to endless rows and moist huddles of the displaced.

Then suddenly the rains stopped. And electricity began to show up for a few hours in the day. The distraught markets were swept clean and the heir of the erstwhile kings gave away a jewel to the river to appease it. His ancestors had prayed at gurudwaras and to the gold-tongued Goddess in the Kali temple whenever the town was in pain, and he did the same. The river accepted the gift and subsided.

Soon only the stink lingered to remind the city of its many losses. A day after I graduated from college, I received a letter from Anna aunty, calling me again to Ambrosa. I refused. I had always gone to Annaville with a sense of hope. Now I had nothing. I knew I would not be able to bear Samir's photograph in his empty room, his raincoat in the kitchen passage, his motorbike leaning against the garage wall.

I would open the drawer of his writing table like a compulsive thief. See my letters and cards stacked and forgotten in a small heap. I would go through his books and linger over the small notes he had scribbled on the margins. I would go through his albums and be hurt by each photo. I would go one day but that day hadn't come yet.

23

I STARTED TEACHING art at a private school. The salary was not great but I stayed busy during the day. At night however, strange dreams flecked my eyes. I often saw Annaville's veranda, and a man waiting in it for me. He was familiar, yet strange. In my sleep, I gave him a face that was not Samir's. Eyes that were quiet and dark. Skin that was permanently sun-scorched. Hair that was closely cropped and shoulders that were square. The stranger rose every time, walked up to me, extended a hand and said, 'Hi. I have been waiting. But it was not yet time.' And I extended my hand and said, 'I don't know why but yes, I have been waiting too.'

He talked to me even during the deep pauses between his words. I laughed at stocky legs. And then I took him to Anna aunty's garden where oil diyas sat on lily pads, fairy lights sliced the sky and candles flickered in sand-filled, brown paper bags lining the pathways. Then my skin turned a creamy crimson and a ruby droplet appeared on my neck. Henna flowered on my palms and stars came down to braid my hair.

We grew silent and the crickets chattered. And then he reached out for me and I for him. In his arms and in my sleep, I vowed each night that I would never remember Samir. Never hurt for a love that was like quicksand. That could be anything or nothing. A love that could have been just a little trick of the senses, an accident, a story I had fed with my lacks. A monstrous weed that should have been plucked out from the root and thrown away.

Then like an echo from the past, Naren uncle arrived in a new car with his daughter's wedding card. His face was a lot like Papu's. Only without the sharp lines and the deep hollows. It was flat and doughy and without any laugh lines.

'Mona, my daughter is going to be married in two days,' he said to the floor. 'I had differences with Veeren bhai . . . he was always too detached from us and Nimmo told me how rude he and your daughter were to her when she came to visit. I don't think, there was any reason for anyone to feel resentful that we moved away to Delhi. There was no future here as Veeren bhai found out. He was in Noida all this while before his death and never contacted us, not even once,' he murmured to the sofa. 'Now all that . . .' he looked at the television, the fridge and the dining table and said, 'is in the past. You are the eldest in the family now. You must come and bless our daughter.' Ma looked at him with large, frightened eyes. Next morning, his driver drove us to Delhi while both Ma and I tried not to remember our last journey to Noida.

Viren uncle dropped us near the elevator of a yellow brick apartment block and said, 'I have to personally invite some guests to the sangeet this evening. Please go up to the seventh floor. First house to the right.'

Nimmo aunty opened the frothing, hot chocolate door and touched Ma's feet. Her skin was bleached, upper lip smooth and shining, eyebrows plucked, hair cut in sharp layers. Her body, however, gave her away. It was big and an upturned belly showed from the distended silk of her embroidered Punjabi suit.

She stretched herself to her full height and screamed, 'Chandraaa! We have guests. Please take their luggage.' A pale girl in a yellow salwar suit emerged from a distant corner and took our suitcases from us. Inside, the walls stepped forward and swallowed us. The jutting wooden cabinets screamed in gold, silver, copper, glass, porcelain voices.

We escaped to the beige sofas and their stack of heart-shaped, purple velvet cushions. The maid appeared again. This time carrying glasses of khus juice. We sipped slowly. Nimmo aunty tapped her feet impatiently. 'How was your journey?' she asked me.

'Fine,' I gurgled out a startled response.

'The car . . . was comfortable? It is new. Bought it just for the wedding.'

'Yes, I seem to remember your passion for cars. You brought one to Patiala too even though we didn't have any garage,' I said.

She looked at the ceiling. We looked too. She explained, 'Those mouldings, we got them finished only last week. We don't want to live in this flat anymore. When we were redoing this place, the neighbours really got jealous. Mrs Chaddha asked me if I was building a palace above her house. I told her, God willing, I would do that one day. Once Mona is married, we will build a farmhouse somewhere.'

She turned to me, 'You are a painter, I suppose? Can you paint a Ganesha mural on my front wall? If you want, we will buy the material.'

'Aunty, we are not going to be here long enough for me to finish the mural even if I get inspired and that seems unlikely,' I answered.

'Ah, so maybe I will buy a Husain and put it up there,' she shrugged.

The doorbell screamed again and Chandra moved quickly to let my cousin Bittu in. He walked in, carrying the swagger of someone who had conjured up prosperity out of the longings of many impoverished generations and made his parents proud with his ability to swish credit cards and air tickets. He was in shorts and a Nike vest.

'Just coming back from the gym in the building,' Nimmo aunty quivered with pride.

Bittu sat down and was served his glass of khus juice.

'So . . . what are you doing?' he cornered me.

'I've just graduated,' I said.

'In what?' he sipped his question.

'Fine arts.'

'I have seen the seven wonders of the world,' he looked at me over his rim.

'Except Taj Mahal,' he finished his juice and got up.

'In that case aunty, maybe, you should get Taj Mahal painted on your wall,' I said as Ma nudged me discreetly.

'What is she talking about?' Bittu asked.

'Come here,' Nimmo aunty opened her arms for him. He bent down and she kissed him on the forehead. 'Mera baccha,' she said to his back.

After he disappeared, she told us, 'Mona is lunching at

Nirula's with friends. She loves pizzas and now of course she can have as many pizzas as she wants in America. The boy is settled in Miami and called her every day!'

Then she rose. 'Let me show you Mona's trousseau,' she murmured.

We followed her to Mona's room. There was nothing in it except suitcases and towers of silks.

Nimmo aunty picked up a large box and lifted its lid and then its misty tissue paper. 'This . . .' she breathed reverentially, '. . . is Mona's wedding dress.' The outfit had a short, gold appliqué bodice and a maroon lehenga where pearls battled with gold flowers for breath. 'Mona saw it in a movie and wanted it. We can't say no to her. Some top designer designed it for her. Ritu something.'

Then Nimmo aunty looked at me with hazy eyes. 'What are you wearing for the wedding? I have something for you. Actually I had bought it for Mona but she didn't want it. You can keep it.'

'Anna aunty sent me something recently. I will wear that,' I said.

'Anna . . .' she murmured with the gold stars still dancing in her eyes. Then the eyes cleared. 'I think,' she waved her hands trying to conjure them back, 'you two must be tired.'

Ma and I slept through Mona's arrival and later spent about fifteen minutes at the ladies' sangeet organised in the lawns of the building. There was a lot of dancing and many food stalls. We sat with our plates and watched flapping silk sails and delirious kurta pyjamas. Mona was a pretty girl. Especially so in her peach and silver saree, but Nimmo aunty's eyes hovered around her like birds flapping their wings in panic. They searched for threatening things everywhere. For earlobes with more diamonds than were studded in Mona's earrings. For taller, better-proportioned frames. For suits with exceptional embroidery. Prettier shoes. It was almost as if her happiness depended on finding things that did not match up to Mona. My hair troubled her a lot.

After the sangeet, when Mona eased into a dewan and let her henna-tinted, shoulder-length hair fall to the carpet, Nimmo aunty saw me looking at her and said with satisfaction, 'Almond oil is the best for hair.'

Then she looked at me with pity, 'You like Chinese food, don't you? I saw you taking a second helping. Well, you can have as much as you want as long as you are here.'

'Actually, I prefer Thai. Anna aunty's cook makes the best Pad Thai ever,' I said.

'Pad . . .?' she fumbled but then continued, 'Go shopping with Mona to the market in our new Contessa. I know life in Patiala has given you very limited exposure but you must experience everything in life. Mona can fit in everywhere because of the exposure we have given her but she has also been brought up with certain values. She is polite to elders and adjustable. She gets along with everyone. She doesn't believe that she is too good for everyone.'

'Good for her, aunty. She must have learnt it all from you,' I smiled.

She frowned at me, 'But you . . . you are going to have trouble. First of all, I don't think, it is so easy to find grooms when you live in a neighbourhood like that. Thank God we moved out when we did. Secondly, how are you going to afford a wedding? Okay, we are there to support but who supported us in our bad times?'

'Don't worry about me aunty. One day, a groom will find me. The question is whether I want to be found. I want to do my Master's in art, first.'

Mona spoke, 'I paint too. I also write poetry. But no one wants me to do anything. One needs encouragement to do all this. Would you like me to do your upper lip?'

24

THE WEDDING WAS held on the grounds of a five-star hotel. I had never really known the joys of dressing for an occasion. Ma had stitched pretty, homely dresses for me when I was a little girl and then my two pairs of jeans and cheap, cotton shirts had hid my youth from the world and from myself.

Anna aunty often complained about my perverse disinterest in my looks. Today I wanted to look beautiful for her. I slipped into a satin-lined jacket, watching with pleasure how dangerously its Chinese collar lit up my face. I held my breath as I stepped into the long skirt of crushed, black silver. I smiled and let my hair loose.

Ma wore an old, blue chiffon. Nimmo aunty looked at me only once during the course of the evening and then never looked again. But she went to Ma with a blue velvet box. 'Would you like to wear some gold? Or a silk saree maybe?' she asked, her face tight with concern. She shrugged when Ma refused.

The evening had a temple theme. Four antique pillars

stood on a baby mountain patched with grass. The pillars were deeply carved and topped by a large rose and jasmine dome. A red silk bolt was bunched up in scallops around the pillars and bouquets of red rose buds hung from every centimetre. Mango leaves ran around the pillars chasing flaming marigolds. Next to each pillar were small pots of receding girths covered in white and red mirror-worked fabric. They fitted perfectly into each other's hollows. The pot towers winked in anticipation.

Two silver chowkis and one aluminium seat covered with cushions awaited the bride, the groom and the priest.

Young banana trees that had arrived at the venue in two trucks were stuck without their roots in the lawns. When dusk fell, fire torches sprang to life. Women in south Indian temple sarees threw flowers at guests. Young, bare-chested men in white dhotis sprinkled gulab jal on guests and served orange, white and black beverages in silver trays.

A shehnai player played desperately on a machaan. In a small stage covered in snowy cloth, a famous ghazal singer belted out wedding songs.

The garden had island tables stacked with food. It was going to be a long ceremony.

A team of video cameramen was taking close-ups of the food. Curries simmered photogenically. Earlier in the day, extreme close-ups of Mona's hennaed hands and feet and her trousseau had been taken.

Everyone had wanted the groom to arrive on an elephant, keeping with wedding theme, but he came in a flower sneezing Contessa.

To herald his arrival, blue and golden litchi lights suddenly lit up the trees and the bushes. People began to dance on the gravel pathways. The shehnai player became frenzied. The ghazal singer stopped because hidden loud-speakers began to emit conch and bell sounds. I could not see the groom's face, hidden as it was behind raining jasmines. Gold and silver covered his turban, his stifling sherwani and his pointed Punjabi feet.

Nimmo aunty looked at him in happy disbelief. Bittu was dancing to Hindi film songs now playing on the speakers, and Naren uncle was sweating in his new blue suit.

All their dreams were coming true. Then Mona arrived in what she had called a 'first ceremony dress'. It was a pink tunic with a gold tissue sharara. A misty gold veil covered the face she had spent retouching for hours in a beauty parlour.

It was sometime before the laughter stopped and she exchanged garlands with her groom.

Tired guests now lounged on white floor mattresses and sipped cool drinks. My eyes were beginning to hurt. I looked away and ran straight into the eyes of a man. I rose and left for a powder room just a short gravel pathway away and wilfully crunched little stones under my heels. Thinking of that gaze, I looked at myself in a large fish-shaped metal mirror in the bathroom and smiled.

When I was walking back, I saw him again. Standing next to a young girl. He was dressed in black. Thin and dark, about Papu's height, closely cropped hair and a boyish awkwardness about him. Especially in the way he stooped painfully to catch the girl's words.

Before I could pass him by, he looked away from the girl and straight at me.

At midnight, a few guests began to leave even though the

ceremony was still going on. Mona was bunched up on her chowki, trying not to fall asleep in her priceless wedding dress. The groom looked ruddy and irritable in front of the raging sacred fire. The priest was explaining the meaning of each wedding shloka in three languages. He obviously loved his job.

We took the morning bus back to Patiala. Within three days, Naren uncle followed us. Over tea, he cornered Ma. 'He is a good boy. A diamond. Your girl is of marriageable age and it is time you stopped consulting her in all matters. I know his family. Gems. All of them. Mother no more. Father, retired civil servant, lives with older son in Canada. That boy has his own business. Gem. They come to India once in two years but won't be able to come for the wedding. Anyway, this boy speaks English as if he were drinking water. He has many proposals so if you delay, you will lose out, not him.'

'Is he talking about my marriage?' I asked Ma.

Naren uncle turned to me, 'Yes, I am. If you lose this boy, you will never find another one like him. Has recently joined a newspaper as sub-editor. Own house. What more do you want?'

'I can't marry all the eligible bachelors in the world,' I snapped.

He shook his head, 'I always felt Veeren bhai saab pampered you too much. Girls, especially in your position, should not have so much to say about anything.'

'What is my position, according to you?' I asked, leaning forward.

He leaned back in satisfaction, 'Are you working? Yes? How much do you earn? 900 bucks? Who is going to support you all your life and give security for old age? Are you going to be a district-collector, a world-famous painter or a prime minister? No. Is any boy waiting for you anywhere? No. Is anyone going to give you anything on a platter? No. Can your mother protect you and watch over you all her life? No. It is time you grew up. Marriage will solve all problems. Your mother will find peace. We don't want our share in this house. God has given us all that we need and more. She can stay here as long as she wants. But you need to get respectably married before people start talking.'

'What will they say? If I refuse to marry this boy?'

'That you are an ungrateful child. You are not getting any younger you know. I know of many girls who turned their noses up at good proposals and then grew too old to get any.'

'I don't want to get married.'

'Why, huh? Look at Mona. Never said anything when we fixed her up. Marriage gives girls everything they need. Financial security. And let me tell you this. That boy liked you. He has recently bought a kitchenette, he is buying things for the house in case you say yes.'

Ma turned to me, 'Meet him once. There is no harm in that.'

'If he wants, let him come here Ma,' I looked away from both of them.

Naren uncle smiled victoriously. 'That is not possible. Girls don't dictate terms in our family. He is a busy man. Working for a newspaper after all. You will have to come to Delhi to meet him.'

I left the room, but in the evening, Ma sat me down and

spoke for a long time. She ended with, 'If your Papu were alive, things would have been different. I have nothing to give you. See him. Say no, but see him once. I know you had feelings for Samir. But he is gone and he will never come back, least of all for you. He didn't care enough to stay or to look back, did he?'

'I just want to build my own life, Ma. You don't need to give me anything.'

'I know he will take care of you and give you something you need. A stable life where you feel safe. If he can inspire so much love in Nimmo, there must be something to him.'

I knew I could fight Naren uncle but I had nothing to battle Ma with. Papu was gone and so was Samir. It was my turn to jump from a ledge like Ma.

25

THE NEWS THAT I had been seen and liked at Mona's wedding had the sweeping wilfulness of a sandstorm. It blew away Nimmo aunty and I wondered if her beige sofas and purple heart-shaped cushions would fly in her wake too. Following her through the windows.

I had somehow disfigured her neat calculations. Her accusing eyes followed me everywhere as if I had stolen a personal piece of fate from her. And ruined partially the thrill of putting her daughter and her many suitcases on a plane to Miami.

I overheard her muttering to her maid, 'She can't walk without a slouch or eat with a knife and a fork. No exposure or sophistication or dress sense. She doesn't even do her upper-lip! And not hospitable either. What will she do in Bangalore? I have seen how small-town people behave in big cities. They act as if they have personally achieved something when they hail taxis and go up and down elevators. Thank God, Gautam works only for a newspaper. He is like a son to us but he doesn't have a car, yet.

Otherwise this one would have exploded with pride.'

When a tea trolley rolled towards me, Nimmo aunty rolled out of the room. But not before throwing a backward glance that said, 'Offer him some tea. And don't mess up my carpet.'

When all was quiet, I heard footsteps. I knew the man who walked in. We had seen each other at the wedding. He sat on a distant ship-shaped, velvet couch I had never noticed before.

I almost chuckled over the vision of him sprouting sails and floating on a marble sea towards me. I knew every room in the house was quietly listening.

'I'll come there,' he said, walking up to me and then, sitting on a sofa inches away from me, said softly, 'Hi, I'm Gautam and well, this place has been like a second home to me. Naren uncle and Nimmo aunty . . . you flinch everytime she talks . . . are not the most discreet or refined of people but they are family and nothing can change that. They were very close to my parents. My mom is no more and my father is abroad, as you probably know. I saw you at Mona's wedding and the idea of getting married was not really something I was consciously considering. But then Naren uncle asked me and I agreed. But of course, you should tell me if this is a good idea for you or not.'

I liked his voice. It fell around me like ribbons of melted chocolate. I felt reassured. Strangely calm. Calmer than I had felt in years. I found myself saying, 'I want you to know something. I was in love. And I am not easy to live with.'

He smiled as if he were reading an easy questionnaire, 'We all have our little stories. But we move on. Don't we?

Should we say yes to them then? Do you want to know my salary?'

I shook my head in panic, violated by the question.

Later, when we were riding towards Qutub Minar on Bittu's abandoned, old bike, Gautam took my hand and put it on his shoulder and said, 'Anytime you want, you can talk. Share everything. Don't be afraid.' I nodded. We talked. About his job and my studies. The living conditions in Bangalore. The house we would live in. His friends. And then there was nothing to talk about. When we passed a big hoarding advertising condoms, I looked bravely at it and wondered.

The next day, in a restaurant full of flower-topped tables, he asked me, 'Are you happy? Yes? Then why don't you smile?'

'This is new,' I smiled at him. 'I just didn't think I wanted to get married now and if you had been a different kind of a guy, maybe I would have said no.'

'Really? So you would have said no to . . .?'

'Hmm, if you were shorter, fatter, if your voice was different. And if you had tried really hard to impress me.'

'Just that?' he asked.

'So far? Yes, just that,' I said and then our chairs were caught in a stream of giggling young girls. And I saw him looking at them. Without any appreciation but with curiosity.

I began to get possessive and resented it when he did not sit next to me at Naren uncle's dining table. His walk was nice. Gentle like his voice. As if he were stepping over puddles. He had gentle eyes and hands too. I didn't ache with him or without him. I liked that. And the sense of peace within him and around him.

I went back to Patiala to re-learn life. To accept that I was not meant for love but for something that fell on my insides like an engine coolant. I began to read women's magazines. Began to cook. And to fry onions evenly on a low flame and boil rajma with star aniseed, cinnamon and black pepper. I bought two cookery books and wrote 'Happy Cooking' on them. And made a scrap book of household tips and recipes.

Every time I heard the word 'Bangalore', a cage opened to set me free. I could see for the first time a man in my future whose face was not barred by shadows. Whose voice was not afraid to call me by my name. I began to write to him. And years of my life rolled into hand-made sheets of paper. He couriered cards addressed to 'My darling'. And I almost turned to look behind me to see whom he meant. I learnt little about him though. Except that he always did what was best for everybody. And that is why he turned down my proposal for a civil marriage in Patiala because he could not hurt Naren uncle. 'He has been like a father to me after Dad moved to Canada. If he wants a certain kind of a wedding for me, I won't resist,' he wrote.

Ma and I began to shop for a trousseau. I climbed the bedroom lofts, opened the lids of the cane boxes she and Papu had brought from Missamari and gently lifted special cocktail glasses wrapped in mothballed, dated newspapers. I gave them one by one to Ma and she cradled them to her heart before putting them in my Bangalore-bound trunk.

She and Papu had a lot to give me. Frosted beer tumblers. Bedsheets and curtains they had bought in Panipat. A mixer-grinder of Japanese origin that Papu had gifted Ma on their last wedding anniversary. And a modest stack of silk sarees that Ma would never wear again. Together we carried the sarees to the Darziyon Wali Gali. It smelt of impending weddings. Behind the glass panes of its trousseau shops, virginal daaj and wari silks gleamed tautly. Waiting to be broken in.

Ma and I walked into a shop where generations of brides on a budget had picked up their wedding dresses. An assembly line of salesmen stretched on a white mattress from one end of the shop to another. 'This is a beauty,' said the salesman facing us when a dress reached him via a few arms. 'A red, silk kurti and ghagara, embellished with gold mangoes. Synthetic gold of course, but no one will know the difference when you wear it . . .' he smiled at me.

I decided to buy it when he wrapped the ghagra around him and struck a pose for Ma and me. Next we went to Masterji's Special Ladies Shop where I sketched designs that could be culled out of Ma's old sarees. Masterji, the head tailor, listened to me with a pencil stuck between his beard and moustache, his turban tilting towards me and his measuring tape rustling like a gentle snake around his neck.

The night he home-delivered the clothes, with 'extra, complimentary' embroidery in one of the suits, I dreamt of the wedding. That I was sitting alone in the marriage mandap. A door opened and Samir walked out of it to stand before me. Then he turned on his heels and went away, slamming the door shut in my face. I woke up with cold fear wriggling in the pit of my stomach. I realised I was shutting all doors through which he could walk back into my life.

On the morning of my wedding, I woke up early and saw Delhi through a fog. I promised the trees I saw from the window that all doors would remain shut to Samir. Anna aunty called to say she was unable to come because Inder uncle was not well. 'Samir would have come but he is unable to get leave,' she said with an unspoken apology in her voice.

In the afternoon, I was bundled into a car and taken to Fee Chu Beauty Parlour. The beautician was of Chinese origin and the walls around her were blue-washed and patched with faces of Hindi film heroines. I had never before seen a beauty parlour from inside and I was curious. I looked at the slightly dusty bank of mirrors before me and caught the proprietress appraising me disapprovingly through them. 'Tch tch, everything is so small. Small mouth, small nose. Eyes, thank God are big. Hair is good,' she said waving a bouquet of black pins in the air.

Then she turned to one of her assistants who was hunched over a cane stool with a tray full of garlic. 'Peel the garlic and mash it with a big spoon.' Then she remembered Ma and turned to her, 'We cook our own lunch here. Do you want a facial? Pedicure? No?'

Soon I was being dusted with powder. I closed my eyes and when I opened them, I saw her reaching out for a box with different shades of blue and red. 'I don't want any colour on my face,' I told her gingerly.

'You *need* colour on your face. Wedding video will look bad otherwise. But if you don't want full bridal make-up, you can have just half. Will cost less,' she said firmly.

'Eyebrows joining in the middle. Never plucked them or what?' she asked irritably, picking at them with a baby tong. Slowly my eyes were lined with silver and blue. Two lip colours were blended in to fill my mouth and make it look bigger. Two shades of brown and yellow foundations were blended with fingertips to give me the 'right complexion'.

'Strange skin. Not like our Mona at all. She is really fair and lovely. Had no problems doing her face,' she grumbled. She draped my red and gold, synthetic lehenga around me and ran an eye-and-a-half over me.

'You can't look so short,' she said and then sat me down.

She piled my hair upon my head and then placed a nest of someone else's hair on top of the heap. 'But ... the colour does not match. My hair is brown. This is black,' I whispered.

'Don't worry. Your dupatta will come on top. No one will notice,' she said and jabbed pins in my head to join the real with the fake.

I saw myself in the mirror but wished I hadn't. I had two faces now. And the two were not seamless. One face looked too brown and the other too white. And there was a green shadow above my upper lip that I had never seen before. My eyes were blue caves and my mouth was a pile of strawberry jam.

'Here,' Miss Fee Chu finished her handiwork by putting a fistful of artificial jewellery around my neck.

Gautam and I were married the same evening in a small community hall. He came triumphantly on a horse with a big sword and garlands made of 100-rupee notes around his neck. The synthetic strands of his sehra glittered in the night. He wore a suit gifted to him by Naren uncle. He looked like a child at an adult party. Happy, incredulous and grateful. '*Deewana ... tera deewana*,' a film song played in the background for the third time in one hour. A girl I didn't know sat next to me and fiddled with my fake nose ring. Bittu walked around in a white suit and smiled once at me. His eyes were moist.

When I was about to put a garland around Gautam's neck, everyone burst into laughter and asked him not to bend down. I stood on my toes and managed to slip it around his neck in the second attempt. Then both of us sat down around a bouquet of flames to be husband and wife. A priest was chanting shlokas. The nose ring was beginning to hurt and my head itched under the fake hair. The wedding I could deal with. It was the hair that was a tragedy. It weighed me down. Made me feel false, and all wrong.

Every time Gautam's hand came into mine, I felt understood. But he was far away. Concentrating on the smoke, the words of the priest, an inner dialogue that I could not hear.

He followed the priest's instructions like an attentive student who wanted to get a test paper right. Ma refused to give me away without Papu so Bittu sat down to fill in for both of them. The rest of the ceremony was a technicolour blur that got over before I could sift familiar faces from unfamiliar ones. I saw very little but could not help watching large mouths in which dahi bhallas, banana moons with imli chutney, baby scoops of ice creams and fried rice disappeared. Gautam and I sat on red and gold chairs on a red and marigold stage and never-ending waves of people swirled around us. We were struck frequently by lightning flashes from a video camera.

'Smile a little madam, you looking too dull,' the video photographer shouted at me from above the fifth instalment of *Deewana, tera deewana*. Women fussed over me. With compliments. And envelopes stuffed with money.

I wanted to be alone with Gautam and to understand the meaning of being married to him. Then I saw Ma sitting across the hall on a lonely chair, seeing me off in her mind. We were brought back to the house with much ceremony in the night. A shehnai player sat on top of our car and played a wedding song as we inched closer to the gate of the apartment complex.

At night, we were told with arched eyebrows and side-long glances that we were to spend our wedding night in Mona's empty room.

'I wish this whole thing wasn't so public,' I whispered to Gautam. 'Couldn't we have gone somewhere by ourselves?'

He smiled indugently, 'They want to do it their way so why create a fuss over one night? We will have all the time and privacy we need in Bangalore.'

So we went into the walk-in wardrobe in Mona's room to change by turns and then sat side-by-side on the bed, he in his white T-shirt and green slacks and me in my cotton nightgown. I turned to face him and he touched my earlobes. His touch was warm. And comforting like that of a faith healer. Then we were holding each other close. Trustingly, like two friends who can laugh at each other without fear.

A little after midnight, Gautam fell asleep. I was still a stubborn virgin and Gautam had not forced matters. My bones felt embalmed with his tenderness. I stayed awake for a long time and for some reason began to remember my first train journey from Asankot to Ambrosa. I wondered if it were raining in Ambrosa now. If the pine trees were wailing.

When I closed my eyes, I felt peace swirling above us in the room, in the mist outside the windows, in the soft sheets we were wrapped in. I was safe. Protected from everything that Samir could now inflict upon me. Everything he would do from now on. It would not matter if he found a woman to love. If he walked past me without looking at me. I had someone who would love me. Someone I would share my life with. No pain would ever lurk outside the door I had closed tonight.

Ma and I sat together for a long time after breakfast. She refused to see us to the airport, so the car drove away, leaving her behind.

Gautam and I sat together on the clouds, with our fingers laced together. 'Where had you hidden yourself all this while? Do you know how lovely you are?' he whispered in my ear, brushing his lips against my lobe. We lunched on fresh fruit, slept close to each other's necks, waiting for the moment when we would reach our home and hold each other close.

26

BANGALORE WAS INSTANT love. Gentle like the thump of a leaf. With traffic jams punctuated by cuckoo calls and drifting flowers that sometimes fell on heated bonnets to calm them down. Traditional like a shloka chant and modern like a busy executive with blocked arteries. Most of all, I loved the trees that grew everywhere and the windows of my new home opened to many flowering rows, to open skies, distant traffic din and squirrels that held up pieces of stale bread and nibbled on them with gourmet grace. Like every other Bangalore neighbourhood, ours too had one staple tender-coconut vendor. From my window I could see him everyday, awaiting customers, leaning against a tree, with pouty tender-coconuts strapped to his rickety bicycle and some heaped around him. He would smile at a regular from a distance and tap the chosen fruit before knifing away its crown in one clean sweep. His large, time-worn knife would carve a little well in the flattened top and then with a flourish, he would insert a cheap straw in it.

After the water had been sipped to the last drop, he sliced

the empty shell in two half-moons and scrapped out dollops of coconut cream. 'Ten rupees only,' he smiled and took the money with his dark-rimmed hands.

Just across him was a pavement piled with watermelons. They lay in green, succulent heaps, soaking in the sun and the sudden showers. Their ruby-red sweetness stopping a young man, possibly a software engineer, in his new car. And a saree-clad woman on her moped. A family of four on a scooter.

And once tempted me enough to walk across and ask for one. The vendor expertly weighed the watermelon he had picked for me, cut a red, fleshy triangle out from the glossy green skin and let me taste it. In one black-salted bite, I tasted summer and the richness of the entire harvest and then drowned in happiness.

Our apartment block in a leafy, middle-class locality had common walls too, like the homes in Bakshi Ganda Singh Street but no one could hear anyone else. I lived a quiet, pre-ordained life in a home which had for some reason been painted pink and green by the family Gautam had bought it from.

So I coaxed Gautam to bring home some paint cans and spent hours standing on a step ladder borrowed from the building's resident electrician, painting and sponging till the house looked like a white and yellow Rajasthani tent. I strolled into a nearby nursery to pick up bougainvillae pots for the balcony, spent hours painting cushions with spring flowers, embroidered dinner napkins and learnt new recipes. I picked up letter- and key-holders and wood roses from Bangalore's pavement vendors and played loud music while cleaning the house and dusting it everyday.

Every morning, when I opened the door to pick the milk packet, I was greeted by a soothing row of rice-flour kolams opposite clean-swept homes. When I tried to replicate them, I learnt that they are drawn not so much with hands as with memory and that each twist and curl of the thumb and the finger is embedded in the genes and each little flower is part of family history. The women who drew them effortlessly probably grew up watching their mothers do the same.

Since the sawdust rangolis I had made during school fests did not belong here, I went and bought myself kolam stickers and dressed up my doorstep with a new one every week.

Gautam had a week before he joined work and we spent one day strolling hand-in-hand through Brigade Road's neon jungle. We sampled five-rupee softees, the smell of cakes in the bustling Nilgiri's supermarket. Inexpensive Chinese food. Beer bars. Steaming idlis and sambhar in a Darshini. Corn on the cob. Pop corn. Export surplus clothes. Ready-made curtains, towels and napkins. Trinkets. Guavas. Track-suits and T-shirts with inane messages. Glitzy music stores. Cheap leather bags. Gautam complained about too little parking space and too many vehicles. I watched young boys and girls in trendy clothes leaning against railings that divided too much wealth from too much poverty. And heard the hum and buzz of a city pleased with where it has come. And where it is going.

Another day, we explored Commercial Street, despite a drizzle that drove us to Anand Sweets where we had one plate each of their luscious gulab-jamuns.

After a few hot dosas at Woody's, when we walked out, I tried holding on to Gautam's arm, but he gently shrugged it away and walked on.

'What is it?' I caught up with him and asked.

'Nothing, I am tired that's all, and I have to join work tomorrow,' he said, starting his bike.

I did believe that nothing was wrong. At least not visibly so.

My red-and-white wedding bangles were taken off by Gautam exactly one-and half-months after the wedding. On the day they were supposed to be taken off. Nothing that was supposed to be done was left undone. I had finally lost my virginity after much patient effort. Gautam never missed special occasions or forgot important dates. On my birthday, he bought me a long skirt and a fitted jacket, took me to a Chinese restaurant and ordered 'Long Life Soup'. We then went to a pub that looked like cramped space ship and to a cinema hall to see Hollywood's freshest disaster fantasy.

My husband, I often said to myself, but the words did not quite sound real. Even though he was real. With toe nails, teeth and chest-hair. And a warm smell that reminded me of roasted cashew nuts. I no longer wondered about condom hoardings and it seemed incredible that *The Complete Sex Manuel* lay on a bookshelf in my house and that it was not out of bounds for me.

It did not seem real that I was now keeping house like a woman. Going with my husband to shops to buy kitchen things. Cleaning cupboards. Washing and sorting male underwear. It was unbelievable that I was married.

When we touched, life became simple and full. And then it grew empty, because except for our bodies, there was little to share.

If I wished to say something, Gautam listened, but never really initiated conversations. Only once, at my insistence, did he speak about his life. His half-hearted crush on a colleague. The loneliness of eating canteen food during the night shift. The joy of having someone now to open the door at night. I asked him once, 'Why did you marry me?'

He said seriously, 'Because the time was right. Because everybody said so. Because I thought you would understand.'

'Understand what?' I asked.

'Me. My life. Considering you have had it pretty rough yourself. My parents divorced when I was about fifteen. I stayed with my mother and my father went to live with my brother. I am hardly in touch with them. Later, when I came here to work, I met Sarita.'

'Why didn't you marry her?'

'Who?'

'Sarita?'

'Her? She and I . . . she was too . . . I didn't want a complicated life. She is very temperamental, demanding . . . she would have spoilt everything.'

'Did you ever . . .? You know . . . with her?'

'*Never*,' he said sternly. Like an insulted virgin.

Gautam occasionally came home from office for lunch. We would eat and then he would yawn. 'I have a double shift today. Will be home late. Must catch a few winks,' he would say and then stretch out on the bed on his stomach, shoe-bound feet dangling from the edge of the bed. I sat quietly and watched him sleep. After an hour, he would drink tea and leave.

Whenever he got a day off, I leaned against him on the motorbike, trying to feel a little of the joy that had evaporated within the first month of marrying him. I tried to grow another person inside me. Someone without expectations. A good cook. House-proud. Eager to please. Gentle seducer. Holding Gautam's back when he slept at night. Stroking his fingers. Trying not to count how many days passed before he remembered me in his bed. His life. Then my body turned away from him. We both grew quieter and to make up for the silence in our marriage, Gautam became even more painfully attentive to my dark moods. I found myself cribbing a lot and was curiously thrilled when he said, 'Ya ... I understand what you feel. I totally understand,' nodding like a successful, prosperous counsellor. He spread like a benign cloud around me whenever I hurt a finger in the kitchen or stubbed a foot against the bed. 'Ohooooo, sssss,' he went, his perfectly shaped lips pursed in concern.

I began to daydream about falling sick, imagining the devotion with which he would nurse me. And then I began to fall sick often. I would often wake up in the night, holding my stomach. And watch with satisfaction as he clucked around me, feeding me glasses of water, milk, vile green antacids, pink gels, herbal mints.

'It was beautiful,' I told Ma over the phone. 'He stood holding my hand when I puked by the roadside after a bad dinner. Any other man would have been repelled. But he stood there, with me. I am so lucky.'

27

IT WAS WHEN I was neither sick, nor throwing up that life stood still. Life was not the charging bull it had been once. I no longer had to grapple with it on mud and get scars and wounds that bled obviously for all the world to see. No poverty. No unpaid electricity bills. No scars of a failed business on the drawing room floor. No violating encounters in streets with grasping young boys. No fire licking at the front door or floods passing me by. No heartbreak. No Papu. No Ma. No Samir.

Now life curled up into a ball of fur and stared blankly at me. It drooled from the mouth. It wanted to be petted once in a while and then it went to sleep with its back towards me. Gautam began to fall into the self-driven rhythm of his bachelorhood. Double-shifts became routine. He warded off my complaints with, 'They all count on me. I can't help it. You want me to leave the job? Just say the word. I will.'

I began looking for jobs, went for a few interviews and then started painting again with a quiet desperation to ease the constriction I felt in my chest.

On a Saturday, when I was carrying out two bulging bags of the week's groceries from the nearby Janata Bazaar, I ran into a couple I had often seen leaving together for work from my balcony.

They took me home in their car with my bags reposing on both sides with the potatoes threatening to pop out any moment.

'Have a cup of tea, then Ravi will escort your potatoes next door,' smiled Zoya. They were a few years older than me and their story stretched across a few weekends.

Zoya occasionally showed me the Bangalore I had missed out on. Like Koshy's, which I did not feel overawed at all by. There was a certain unhurried languor about the place, and when you stepped inside, the day slowed down, as did your breathing and time. A waiter ambled up to you with a frayed menu and spread out a chequered cloth on the table. Rearranged the salt and pepper shakers.

Zoya and I often ordered toast and tea at Koshy's and spent some time soaking in the gentle din and the regulars. A foreigner sitting alone with fish and chips. The television reporter and her friend pouring out coffee and conversation. A journalist interviewing an artist. A playwright jotting something in a writing pad.

Zoya had grown up in Delhi, in a traditional Muslim family. Everything went wrong when she met Ravi in college. 'You always believe that you are brave till something like this happens. It took me so long to accept that I had fallen in love with a Hindu boy! He knew right away that he wanted to marry me. The first time we went for a movie, I was so fidgety, we had to leave after twenty minutes. He dropped me two blocks from my house and kissed me on the mouth, in this matter-of-fact way, and drove off! That did it for me! Really no looking back after that, but I was still scared to death. And he had his own problems: his father is a politician, and not just any politician. He thinks Muslims are going to take over India because they breed too much. He wants a pure Hindu nation cleansed of a Muslim gene-bank,' laughed Zoya.

On our pot luck night, as we ate her Hakka noodles with my fried potatoes, she continued, 'It got really ugly. Someone saw me with Ravi and his friends at a birthday party and told my parents about it. When I came back, I was beaten up at home by my brothers. Then I guess, word reached his father too. Because that night in 1984, when Sikhs were being killed on the streets, his father sent some of his men to our house. They came with choppers and tyres and kerosene. When so many Sikhs were being killed, a few Muslims along the way could not have complicated matters. There was a curfew on and so no one came to help when our house was torched. Luckily, we were at a neighbour's house because they had forced us to camp there for the night. But my parents threw me out when they saw their house go up in flames. Ravi and I left town after a week.'

I came back home that night, feeling my home gnaw at me with sudden nails. I remembered Ravi and Zoya's walls covered with big photos frames celebrating their escape to life. Photos where they kissed, unaware of the camera. Where they posed in malls. Were neck-deep in blue oceans.

Gautam came home from work with an unfamiliar glow on his face. 'Sarita insisted on coming over for dinner tomorrow night and I could not say no—she's my bureau chief! Must warn you though, she's a bit fussy about everything so try and keep it simple. Just make some sprouts, yellow dal and stuffed rotis with very little oil and ... and a nice dessert to round it all off?'

I was mildly curious and wanted to see why my husband's face grew brighter when she called. Why he was unable to look at me after each call. Why his shoulder shrugged my hand off at night. Why he had gently pushed me away at Commercial Street during the first week of our marriage.

The moment I saw Sarita, I knew that the hard, jam-topped, orange pastry in the fridge was a mistake. I had picked it up from a multi-coloured bakery shop full of blotchy bread loaves and green-and-pink cakes, stiffly iced with vegetable fat. She was tall and dark and smelt of something expensive and the rain that was just beginning to fall outside. She held me with long slim arms and said, 'She is beautiful ... which tree did you pluck her from?'

I knew also that I looked excessively layered in my magenta Patiala salwar before her clean-lined sarong skirt and spaghetti top. Before her wide, curious gaze, the artificial pearls from one of Patiala's shops itched on my neck uneasily. Even Ma and Papu's special melamine dinner-set looked chipped and apologetic.

Sarita smoked determinedly, as if to prove a point to me, and her eyes did not leave my face. She stuck her fork in the pastry and pretended to fight with it and then left it alone. She talked a lot.

I looked at Gautam and he seemed to have retreated to an island far away from the sound of her voice and from me. He was busy forking down his pastry.

I caught Sarita looking at him indulgently, 'Just look at the way he wolfs down his food! It's a joke in office and everyone stops to watch him when he is eating!'

'I will just step out and get some hot chocolate fudge for you both,' Gautam rose hurriedly and then Sarita and I were alone.

After a moment, she resumed the conversation, 'Does he do that baby talk at home? He really is funny when he gets in the mood, which isn't often, I admit.'

'He laughs, yes,' I said, almost defensively.

'Do you give him tea in the morning? He told me you make good tea.'

'Not any more. He makes it himself because I can't brew it the way he does.'

'I know, he is fussy about little things and not so much about the things men usually get worked up about, like frayed clothes and bad omelettes. Money is an issue with him though, isn't it? Actually, he was supposed to get a big raise this year but it didn't happen. He told me you like nice things and it is obvious from the way the house looks now.'

'I am looking for a job and I don't really spend any money on myself. I do like to keep a good house and he hasn't told me not to,' I said in a tight voice.

'No, no, don't get me wrong, but there is no harm at all in being a bit careful with money. I get your point about the house, but small savings can help you in big ways. Gautam was telling me, you miss your mother a lot and talk to her constantly. Well, if you call your mother only after eight in the night, you cannot even imagine how much money you will save him. He asked me the other day where he could buy you a loofah from. You wanted one, right? Well, his bathroom floor is pretty rough so how about scrubbing your heels on it? Ha ha . . . just joking. Sometimes I just talk too much.'

'You do.'

'Oh, before I forget,' she stuck a cigarette in her mouth and pulled out a small box from her wet, red leather bag. She opened the box slowly like it was a family secret. A pair of pearl earrings and a pendant lay like a cluster of raindrops inside.

'These are real,' she said and then pointed at my neck. 'You can chuck the fake ones out now if you want.'

'Mine are real too, but only to me because my father bought them for me.'

She laughed, 'I am a little blunt. Don't mind me. I just feel too strongly about certain things. I can never shut up when it comes to Gautam. He is right here,' she thumped her heart and smiled. 'I just expect his wife to live up to him in every way, that's all,' she said and rose as Gautam entered the room holding two Corner House bags.

After she left, the kitchen sink got clogged and Gautam came in to the kitchen to hold my shoulders from behind and to say above my ear in a bruising, gentle tone, 'Did you notice how articulate she is? She is pretty reserved usually so I was surprised that she hugged you. Well, everything went well but please, never buy that pastry again. It was awful.'

Maybe it was the sink or just the combined ache of the last few weeks, but I burst into tears and heard Gautam from the distant island he had retreated to earlier in the evening, 'Why are you crying? What happened to the sink? It's alright, I will call the plumber tomorrow. Oh God, what happened?'

Ten minutes later his soft, self-congratulatory snores filled up the night. As if whatever the day expected of him had been delivered.

28

THE NEXT MORNING, Gautam served me breakfast in bed and held me till the trees outside the bedroom window turned white hot in the sun. When he left, I began to clean the house, singing to myself.

Sarita called in the evening, 'You two are having dinner with me tonight. Just returning the favour. I am also calling some of our friends over. See you at seven. Tell him to wear those gold cuff links I gave him.'

Later, sitting behind Gautam's bike, I felt Bangalore's night lights like pangs and wished I could be the man speeding away on a bicycle just ahead of us in a T-shirt that boasted, 'I run on my own fuel'.

Sarita's terrace flat had a good view of the city. Once in a while, I turned back from the night sky to watch her. Her hair was open. As was her saffron shirt till her flaring collar bones. She wore a jade skirt with a ruffled, uneven hem, and I could see her ankles waiting like watchful snakes near my feet. Her arms moved in the night air, scooping the stars, sprinkling invisible confetti. Their tan gleamed with gold dust. Her eyes were moist with the wine she had been drinking. I could not see Gautam in the crowd but I could hear him laughing. Louder, more freely than I had ever heard him laugh at home.

There were too many people. A pony-tailed man sat on a beanbag with a woman on his lap. Whenever there was laughter, both of them shook in tandem and his hands travelled to her giggling breasts to contain them.

Two girls walked up to me and congratulated me in whispery, talcum-soft voices. One of them said, 'Have you met Sarita?' Her eyes were chatty and curious.

'Yes, she came home for dinner,' I answered.

The two girls exchanged a quick glance and one of them asked, 'And?'

I shrugged, 'And?'

'I mean, what happened? Did she behave?'

'How was she supposed to behave?'

'Oh, you know, she has been acting bizarre from the time Gautam got engaged. What did she say to you?'

'Nothing that mattered.'

They looked disappointed and left.

Through the evening, I saw several curious glances measuring me from head to toe.

There was loud laughter and jokes I did not understand immediately. 'So does Gautam try different flavours every night?' a man with a goatee and curly hair smirked.

'Flavours? He does not like ice-cream that much,' I answered, and through the laughter and cat-calls that rocked the room, I saw Sarita's face. It looked disfigured, as if she were going to throw up any minute.

A man standing next to me suddenly swooped down,

pecked me on the cheek and laughed. Thankfully, the attention shifted to a few couples pounding the floor. Hours later, when the music waned, Sarita orchestrated some silence with her hands, 'Sshh, everyone. Let's not forget why we are here. Gautam is a married man now. Married,' she pointed her glass at me, 'to her!'

Gautam was watching her and I watched him. I saw for the first time, eyes that belonged to him, not to the apologetic, self-effacing person he was trying to be to fit around my edges. Sarita returned his gaze and then looked at me, 'He is all hers now. Though, I do wonder if they try something more adventurous than just ice-cream!'

There were more titters and cat-calls and one of the girls who had spoken to me earlier in the evening raised an eyebrow at me and winked conspiratorially.

After all the guests had left, Sarita flopped on a futon and watched Gautam rid the room of chilli kebab burps and cigarette smoke with an air-freshener.

She said to no one, 'He always was too naïve to fall in love. I always knew he would have an arranged marriage because love . . . now isn't it dangerous to love someone with all your heart, Gautam?'

He did not answer her and she continued, 'Love brings with it a hunger, not just for each other's organs. I have always known that you can hold a person's organs but not him. I wouldn't know how to make love to a stranger.'

Gautam watched her and me as if he had ice cubes in his mouth that would fall out if he said something.

Sarita stretched like a cat and looked at me. 'Do you love him?' she asked.

'Saru,' Gautam said in a quiet, measured tone.

'Don't go home tonight, Gautam,' she said, pinning him to a cushion with her eyes.

I watched them in silence. 'I . . . we have to. It's very late,' Gautam spoke gently.

'What will you both do at home? Don't go. Not tonight,' she leaned forward with tears beginning to moisten her lashes.

'Alright,' Gautam rose, 'we can sleep in the guest room. I have had too much to drink anyway.'

I rose to follow him but Sarita reached out to clasp my hand and whispered, 'Don't follow him in. Don't disturb him. He is too drunk and too tired to play the groom today.'

'You know Sarita, I am too sleepy to care where I crash. I would follow him in if I really wanted to, but I won't. I know that you really want to, but can't.'

The shock on her face passed quickly as she spread out the futon and stacked two cushions at one end, 'There,' she sighed, and then she switched off the light and went into her room. I heard her door shut.

It was clear by now to me that the battle, if any, was between Sarita and Gautam. And that it was upto him and not me to finish it.

I fell asleep uncomfortably and resentfully and it was dawn when I tiptoed into Gautam's room. He mumbled, 'Where were you? In the loo?'

I went back to the futon without answering him.

In the months that followed, my bravado faded away because there was no one to direct it against. I was working part-time as a hobby teacher in an evening school and the routine was reassuring. Something was wrong though, because I often misplaced the house keys, left curries on the cooking range and came back from a walk to find live coals in a saucepan.

Nimmo aunty called once to say, 'Some people have become too big to remember us. It is good that you have a man like Gautam because no one else would have been able to handle you and your carelessness. Start taking almonds to improve your memory. Gautam tells me you look unhappy. Why do you look unhappy? Remember your life in Patiala and how many years you spent without a toilet with a flush?'

'Yes, aunty, thank God for the flush in my pretty toilet, otherwise I don't know where everything would have gone. Maybe I would have directed it to your designer bathroom in Delhi.'

There was a pause on the other end and then came an incredulous click as the phone disconnected. I smiled, but then felt a sudden panic at the thought that perhaps I was changing and not for the better.

I had begun to shout at Gautam for no obvious reason while he sat hunched on a sofa, looking devastated. He sneaked in and out of the house when I was in a rage and then, one day, just like that my anger lost its explosiveness and turned into a terminal detachment. I began to remember things I had forgotten.

The compounded smell of agarbattis and sweet rasgullas at Missamari's cinema hall canteen. Anna aunty's veranda smelling of spring and the curly fumes of Tortoise mosquito coil. Succulent samosas and kachauris fuming in oil-filled karahis in Patiala. A bougainvillea bush that Ma had taken from Anna aunty and put on our terrace next to Papu's lonely Noida plants. Its pink and magenta flowers crawling over a parapet to greet visitors when they walked into Bakshi Ganda Singh Street. The glinting, silver-peppered, smooth-sanded water surahis in a potter's shop in Sarhindi Bazaar. Swishing beards, incense haze, green, satin chadars, marigold strings, fistfuls of puffed rice and sugar balls in the box-shaped mosque in the compound of Malwa cinema hall. The days and nights when I knew who I was and where I belonged.

The smell of life in my life when I was falling, painfully in love. The smell of roses opening in Annaville's morning garden. The smell of Annaville. Not its flawless walls or the polished floors, alternately cool and warm under my feet. But the smell that told me that for some people like Anna aunty, life was complete. Well-dusted. Cobweb free. Organised in neat, fragrant halves that fitted into each other perfectly. I missed myself in Annaville. I missed the youth I had missed. I missed being in love and in pain that could be dealt with because they came from a source I recognised. I missed desire. Missed being open to magic. To days when Samir and I had had the choice to be together or be apart. When we were not just part of each other's history but had walked through gardens, driven past tea gardens, locked eyes and smiles and frowns and loved and hurt each other with all of our life stretching before us. I missed the hope that, one day, we would discover a way to find each other, untangle our angry knots and hold each other forever.

Sometimes, while painting, I looked out of the window at a rectangular night and saw a large bandicoot thumping across the silent road. I saw coconut trees with sleepy fingers and heard their moans. I saw the house around me. Yellow and white walled, white-tiled, filled with longings and painted cushions and our bed sheet blotched with Gautam's morning tea. Then I thought of Gautam. The silver-gray silhouette of his back when he slept at night. The silhouette slowly rocking to the pulse of his soft snores. The stoop in his shoulders when he poured over the morning papers. The edgy voice with which he complained about a sub-editor's mistake. The pulpy sounds that he made when he ate mangoes. The big mouthfuls of chicken he ate. The close-lidded faith with which he lit an incense stick in the morning. The two-minute jog he did on the carpet we had bought from a roadside stall. The soggy newspapers on the towel railing in the bathroom. His wordless kindness. His unspoken promise that he would be there to see me suffer and suffer with me but never think of freedom for us both as a possible life choice. His unfailing courtesy in saying good morning and goodnight and bye. His gaze that never saw me or through me but a woman who was not what she was supposed to be. Who was supposed to fit gratefully into moulds but did not. His threatening patience that said, 'One day you will understand'. The stab of tenderness I felt when he drove away on his bike, wearing one of his denim shirts.

I did not, could not remember any words he had said to me. They had disappeared. I did not even remember when it had begun. The estrangement of gaze and touch and thought. I remembered only that I had slept with my hand close to his on the pillow hoping that he would hold it. The few times he had and the many times, when I had held him and he had brushed my hand away with exquisite politeness, sapped perhaps by earthquakes, train crashes, fires and famines around the world.

I was drawn occasionally to a freshly-built temple in the neighbourhood where pomegranate trees circled unfinished and grainy walls, possibly waiting for the last sponsored layers of plaster.

Outside the temple, a woman with dark, full cheeks, paan-stained lips and a big bindi sat, selling flowers. 'Take something Amma,' she called out to my back every time, and one day, I stopped. Her name was Shanti and she sold flowers in the evening and, during the day, hawked loose cigarettes, vegetables, wood-roses, black jamuns, peaches or lychees on Bangalore's pavements. She was the sole bread-earner of her family and fed an alcoholic husband, two young sons and a baby daughter. She ran the fastest behind the local bus. And fought the hardest for her seat. As she measured out a jasmine garland for me, she said, 'One has to be persistent and loud in the world, Amma. Otherwise no one stops. When I call out, "Amma, the freshest roses, the best garlands", I am heard.'

Inside the temple, it was comforting to sit before the gleaming, peace-dispensing gaze of Vishnu and Lakshmi and to watch the priest swing his little bell and revolve a lamp-lit thaali before the Gods. I tried not to see an elephant-legged man, spending the last days of his life here, slivering coconuts with a crescent knife. The cotton tufts on his skull told me that my life, unlike his, was yet to be lived, but the thought fell unnoticed and fluttered like a wisp of hair out of a window.

On my way back from work, I began to notice how the

back flaps of autos cheerfully called out to me with 'Jesus Loves You'; 'Jesus Never Fails'; 'Smil plis'; 'If it is to be . . . it is up to me'; 'God bless you'; 'Use your life'. One evening, a perky car bottom whizzed past me, inscribed with a personal message from someone, 'Caring for you always . . .' And then a door opened and a thought tip-toed into my dark emptiness. Was this message from Samir? What if he was alone too? Feeling me like a vacuum in his insides? And suffering? Feeling raindrops on his mouth and shivering with unresolved kisses? What if, like me, he too travelled from one wet, leafy avenue to another, hoping to see me?

And then I began to see him everywhere. Sometimes at a traffic signal. On a bike. In a stranger's caramel jacket. I heard his voice above the traffic din. Felt his breath at my throat. Heard messages from him on the radio. I opened magazines and books feverishly and read things he wanted me to know, 'Live before you die. Start something new'. Sunset-red film posters of young couples in a laughing embrace made me ache and I wondered how we would pose for a picture together if, by some miracle, we found each other someday. He would stand behind my back, clasp me in his arms, rest his chin on my head. And I would lean back against his chest. Cross my arms and hold his. Feel his smiles with the back of my head.

29

'COME WITH ME to Infant Jesus; I try and go there every Thursday in my lunch hour,' Zoya said over the phone one day, so I went along to pay him a visit in his sleepy, blue dome.

The dust-brown road to the church was bordered with kiosks selling candles, flower garlands, Baby Jesus pictures and Plaster-of-Paris statuettes. Tarpaulin sheets were spread out on the edge of the road and piled with miniature sofa sets, ceramic pottery and dirt-cheap bananas. Vendors briskly sold green guavas, raw mango slivers and ripe jackfruit secrets. Inside the church, misery and hope roared silently. A long human chain carried burning candles towards the pedestal of the benignly varnished, brocade-, lace- and electric bulb-clad Infant Jesus. The benches in the middle were packed with whispering devotees. A woman knelt, her face creased with the passion of her grief. Another, in a burqa, looked quietly, beseechingly, at a God she was not supposed to pray to. People prayed wordlessly, shielding their candles from the wind.

Melted dollops of wax fell on unflinching hands while eyes remained closed, lips murmured vows and troubles, hearts beat feverishly with fear and love. I felt unburdened. As if something had been taken off my shoulders and distributed among all the people in the church. The lightness lasted for a few days before I began to wonder once again about days falling off the calendar. About misery without a cause.

As they usually did, Zoya and Ravi dropped in unannounced one evening to bundle me in their car to take me for a movie.

'The area is not pretty but we will get tickets easily here,' Zoya apologised for the squalor of the locality we drove into. The cinema hall stood right in the middle of two sharply-divided halves. One-half comprised a small temple, a police station, a few self-respecting apartment buildings and a prosperous New Taj Mahal restaurant with a young boy tossing a rumali roti by an open-air food kiosk.

The other half reeked of dank butcher shops with screens of glossy, varnished goat innards. The area was redeemed by a small mosque with a neatly painted green dome.

The cinema hall stood next to a gaudily-painted, pedestal-mounted statue of Dr Ambedkar. The two halves knew their religion but those living around the Ambedkar statue were not too sure about theirs. They were also too poor to care.

The lobby of the cinema hall had Plaster-of-Paris women in Ajanta postures. They all held empty pots in their stubby hands and looked blankly with their gray-white gaze at the people who streamed in. The seats inside had broken spines and sagging bottoms. 'The cola is semi-warm, the samosas are hard and the popcorn is damp. It all fits,' giggled Zoya.

When the movie started, the hall burst into a lusty roar, which got deafening when Shah Rukh Khan began to dance. Like Papu's Dilip Kumar, he was a Muslim, but times had changed. He could be a star now without adopting a Hindu name. The heroine with him was beautiful. The edges of her hair were singed by light. Her cut-glass cheekbones were aflame. Their love song was not yet over when people in the lower stalls began to talk. First softly. And then loudly.

A few men rose and started to move around. We left our seats unwillingly to look down from our balcony. There was chaos in the pit down below. A man shouted at us, 'Riots outside. Stay where you are.'

Within minutes the lights came on and the screen turned white. A child began to cry behind us. A Sikh family stood up. They didn't know their status in the middle of what was possibly a Hindu–Muslim riot. A man I had seen at the ticket window strolled in casually. 'All of you should just sit down and watch the movie. Where will you go? They are pelting stones and bottles outside. Sit still. Nothing will happen. This happens all the time, whenever a fool throws a cow's tail in a temple or a pig's head in a mosque, but then nothing really happens. Things are worse now because of what may happen in Ayodhya. But don't worry. The police station is just across the road. Eat your popcorn.'

Zoya spoke hoarsely to Ravi, 'I want to go home.'

Her voice cut through the foot-shuffles, the worried whispers and crackling popcorn packets. 'They'll come in with kerosene cans and matchboxes and tyres, knives and choppers and hooch bottles and they'll cut us all in half and then set us on fire. I want to go home. I want to go home. Take me home now.'

Ravi was sweating but he managed to say, 'Sshh ... Bangalore is not ... that place. Don't frighten everybody. They are all like us here.'

She slumped back in a seat with her face in her hands. The lower stalls were in a heaving frenzy by now. Somebody was shouting. I caught sight of man looking in panic at a burqa-clad woman with a baby. 'Why do you have to wear so many bangles at night?' he was screaming.

Zoya got to her feet and took Ravi's hands, 'Let's go home. I am not scared now.' She looked at me, 'If they're Muslims, I will say you are with me. If they're Hindus, you say the same.' I nodded.

Her eyeballs were dilated as if she were watching a nightmare in her sleep. I felt grateful that she was dressed in jeans and a block-printed kurta. I never wore my mangalsutra. We did not look too different. She could pass off as my elder sister. It was going to be easy.

We began to walk towards the exit and others followed too.

Slowly we all filed past the cheerfully glowing cola-vending machine, the silent popcorn machine, the glass-encased movie posters, the stink from the bathrooms. We walked carefully down the sweeping staircase. No one wanted to die in a stampede.

The night air was quiet and gentle and well-intentioned. We broke into a run towards the parking lot.

'It is safe,' breathed Ravi. Zoya left my hand and smiled faintly at him.

I saw some decapitated bottles lying near the compound wall, and smelled smoke. My head swung in its direction. I saw a bonfire, made of a few tyres. Then I saw them. They were running silently towards us. Like a pack of yellow-eyed, black jackals. They had bottles and butcher knives in their hands. They were following the enemy, and it was just too bad that we were in the way. 'You two run! I will try to get the car ... *go!*' Ravi screamed.

A few seconds later, I realised I was running alone towards the police station.

The building was intentionally dark. It did not want to be a refuge. Two men in khakis stood near the gate. 'Don't come here ... don't come here,' they screamed in terror. 'We can't do anything. We have called for more people. Till they come, nothing can be done. Go home. Don't come here.'

One of them swung a baton wildly at me. I ducked and ran again towards what looked like a marathon stream of men, women and children running towards lights they could not yet see. A car stopped next to me. When I was pulled inside, I noticed Zoya.

We were silent till we got home.

The phone was ringing when I entered the house. It was Sarita. 'Gautam can't come on the phone right now, but he told me to tell you not to worry. It's too unsafe for him to come home on his bike and there's curfew in the city. My place is closer to the office and I will take him with me in the press van. Your area is notorious for arson ... what if the van is stopped or attacked?'

Gautam came home the next afternoon after the curfew was lifted.

He looked frazzled and apologetic, his eyes futile like searchlights with faint batteries, and said, 'I wanted to come home but Sarita ... you know how insistent she can be. She threw a fit and that too before everyone in office and the best thing seemed to not make a scene. I had no choice.'

'Don't worry, I won't make a scene either,' I said and went to the kitchen to cook. He sat on the sofa with his head bowed down for some time and then switched on the TV.

Life lapsed back to its frightening, unresponsive tranquillity.

One weekend, I decided to go to Koshy's on my own. I reached Shivajinagar in a bus and began walking through its pre-Christmas festivities towards M.G. Road. Shivajinagar nutshelled a city that did not know its religion and yet knew them all. But there was a charged heaviness in the air. Ayodhya's angst, though thousands of miles away, was seeping into Bangalore too. Hand-written posters beseeched peace. Huddles of Muslim auto-drivers discussed what might happen when a rath yatra of Hindus descended on Ayodhya and the mosque.

I spent an hour at Koshy's and then walked to an old theatre that had once hosted British revellers in its opera gallery. I bought myself a matinee ticket and sat alone to laugh through a silly comedy. Feeling better than I had in months, I walked back to Shivajinagar and boarded a bus. From the window, I watched the sun slowly turn red behind the trees. Suddenly, I felt the conductor's hand tap my shoulder. I hunted for a five rupee note in my bag and gave it to him. 'No change,' he rasped.

'I don't have change either,' I blinked and turned away from him. I just wanted to look at the sun.

Then I felt his breath on my ear, 'Look at me when I talk to you.'

Something about him made me remember the condoms left in our tin letter-box after Papu's death. And the hands reaching out to grab my breast. The man was now peering hard at my face. I wondered if he was drunk and whispered, 'I don't have change.'

'I know why you don't have change,' he came closer and I could smell something vile on his breath.

His eyes were peering straight into mine when he said, 'You don't have change because your daddy is a bastard.'

I got up and only when the bus stopped, did I realise I had slapped him.

The man was holding the back of a seat. His eyes were white and his face had disappeared in them.

I heard the crack after my face exploded. I saw his fist coming down again and then I screamed, 'You will pay for this. My husband is a journalist.'

The men and women in their seats were just white dust. The kind that swirled around Ma's feet when she had walked from Lahore towards the Indian border.

One of my eyes was just red haze and my mouth felt strange as if I had swallowed a large balloon. A woman picked me up from the middle of the aisle and said, 'Get down. Don't create trouble.'

'I won't get down,' I screamed.

The conductor came to life again. His eyes were glowing with joy. He spat at me and threw out my bag, my broken, limp watch. And then he pushed me out.

'I will go right now to the police and have you arrested,' I said through a mouthful of blood.

He leaned against the door and smiled, 'Police? Don't you know what they do with girls like you over there?'

Then the bus waddled away. Its shaking bottom laughing at my face.

An auto driver materialised and fumbled in his pocket. With his starched white handkerchief pressed to my mouth, we sped through the traffic to the nearest hospital. When we stopped, I gave him his handkerchief back and tried to open my bag. He shook his head, 'The meter wasn't on, Amma. Don't bother.'

He walked me through thick walls of human stench and seated me on a stool before someone looked me over. When my face was half-covered in a bandage, a hand gathered me up, my bag, took me to a payment counter and helped me back in the auto.

'Where to Amma, let me take you back home?' All through the journey, the auto driver spoke in compassionate Kannada. At home, I dialled Gautam's office number. He came on the line chewing something. His computer keyboard rattled in the background.

'Yes?' he said.

An hour later, he was standing before me with disbelieving eyes. 'What is this?' he asked again and again in different, whispery tones of compassion.

'*What* is this?'

'What is *this*?'

'What *is* this?'

I asked him, 'Your newspaper can't do anything? They hit a woman in a public place.'

Gautam touched my wounds with feathery fingers and shook his head, 'I checked with my editor before coming here. The paper does not want to get involved with something potentially dangerous. And with the Ayodhya tension, it might take a Hindu, Muslim or a north Indian–south Indian angle.'

He shook his head again. 'Anything could have happened today. And when you are travelling in a bus, you should try not to speak in Hindi. Not all people here like north Indians. They think northies are trouble-makers and fighter-cocks. I don't blame them.'

'Do you think I misbehaved with that conductor?' I asked him.

He shook his head, 'Well, you definitely overreacted. You should just have got off the bus and taken an auto.'

When I woke up at night, I knew he wasn't there. He had left a note. His newspaper was monitoring the situation in Ayodhya round the clock, he'd written, and he had to be there to edit various reports.

I put the note away because it did not matter whether he was there or not. My breathing calmed down along with the blood in my veins. The pain in my bruises eased up. I tottered to the cupboard and took out a bottle of sleeping pills that Gautam had once retrieved from Sarita's bathroom cabinet. I took it back to the bed and settled comfortably against the pillows.

I watched a silent film play itself out on the blank wall opposite and ate the pills like popcorn. I was in Patiala. Walking towards my house. I knocked at the old, well-worn wooden door but a stranger opened it. It wasn't Papu. He wasn't anywhere. I ran to the bridge to look for Ma, but she was busy watching the shadow of a hollow moon in a dead river.

I ran to Ambrosa. I ran along the Perfect Eight, but it's symmetry had been broken. Now it was a long serpent curling on and on. I could not see Annaville. Only unfamiliar houses. Strangers. Then I was running down a slope towards Annaville, and Samir was watching me from the veranda. He opened his arms and said, 'Darling'. Before I could reach him, he turned away and disappeared.

I was Ma and walking with ghosts in a caravan of shadows. With nothing and no one waiting for me in the future. I covered myself with a white sheet and stretched out on the bed and looked at the ceiling till it became darker and darker. Sometime later that night, I heard the doorbell. The movie had stopped playing a long time back. The wall was a deathly white. I heard the bell again and knew I had to get up. If I got up and opened the door, I would live.

I suddenly realised it was crucial to live.

I had to live. For myself.

And for the little girl from Lahore who had walked endless miles so she could grow up and bring another life to this world.

For the woman who stood on a bridge and did not jump because I had stirred within her.

The bell was screaming now. I tried to get up but my legs had melted away. I held on to the walls and floated. Sometimes I fell and then got up and then fell again.

But I opened the door and then Gautam held me. I fell asleep instantly but woke up occasionally to find he was running with me in his arms. It must have been very late because there was no one on the roads except us and the curious dogs who sniffed me every time Gautam stopped to breathe.

Then I was in a sterile, hospital bed and could not feel the clothes on my body. All I could feel was the bitter popcorn congealing in my stomach and then flying out from my mouth in minor explosions. I held on to the sides of the bed and fought to spit death out of my body. Then I slept.

30

PAPU STOOD NEXT to me. Together we looked out of the hospital window. Together we both laughed at the foolishness of mourning the dead.

He said, 'I never left. I watched the both of you all the time. When she slumped into the sofa after you told her, I didn't need to hold her because you did. You did me proud. I heard you singing in the bathroom. My favourite ghazal! And to think you never sang it to me when I asked you to. I did spoil you too much, didn't I? But I felt so proud when you held your mother before the pyre. I heard all of Rani's thoughts. She was thinking of the hollow in the pillow next to her. She was thinking of my arms. She was thinking of the laughter. The anger. The poverty. The scooter rides in the rain. The richness of loving the way we did. She was thinking of the whiskey bottles on the trolley. Of the bottle opener. She was thinking of all my songs. I know she never trusted anything or anyone except me. When I went, her link with life broke and that is why she began to fear everything. That is why she asked you to marry Gautam.

Don't hold it against her. She just wanted to protect you. From something. She did not know that no one can protect anyone from life. From living their destiny. From being who they are meant to be. You cannot escape from life. It won't let you escape. It will find you. And when it does, you can either stay or you can run a few more miles till it finds you again. Choose. You tried to hide. To run. Always. What do you fear so much? When you learn to trust, you will learn to live. I want you to tell your mother something. Tell her that she only has to reach out. She will find me because something survives death—us; what we mean to each other. Pain, grief, losses come and go. Only fools embrace them and make them their most trusted friends and keep them alive with sad words and feed them with memories. It is foolish, this holding on to pain, because one day, it will grow larger than your hopes, your joys and it will destroy you. Tell her that there is only one constant. The fact that we loved.'

I heard him but only just. I was swimming in the relief of knowing that he was not dead. Never had been. That his heart had not burst open in pain. That he was well. He wore his tweed blazer. His hair had a little more salt than pepper now. He was alive. Somewhere.

I told him, 'You know Papu, I have always lived with real things. Real people. Real pain. Real anger. Life and death. I have been alive. I never wanted anything. Just to be alive like you. But now nothing seems real. I share nothing with anyone anymore except space. When I see Gautam, I am conscious of nothing except the space between us, around us, below us, above us. I feel I am trapped in a room full of cotton. When I walk, I sink. I hear nothing but the ticking of the clock, wasting seconds, minutes, hours, years of my life. I only wait . . .'

Papu shook his head, 'That is no excuse for doing what you did.'

I took his hand, 'I know. But you don't know what it is to live with nothing. I was so tired after you went. And then Samir went. I don't blame him. He had to. We all have to live the lives meant for us. Then Ma found Gautam. I felt safe with him. We both felt safe in our marriage. Like two people sitting in a living room, bundled up in life-jackets and combat helmets, watching TV and letting life go by outside their windows. Marriage took away the fear of being hurt. Gautam never hurt me because he couldn't. But he took away my sense of living. The day I married him, my body, my heart and my mind—all began to chatter in different languages. I gave myself up to find nothing. Gautam has a lid for himself but I want to breathe, now. To look at the sunset and smile. Watch the moon when it sheds silver shadows on the road without feeling sad. And I want . . .'

Papu was quiet.

'Papu, I want my body back. I couldn't feel it, even when I was dying. I felt as if I ended at my neck. Marriage labelled and delivered it to Gautam, his ancestors, his heirs by a ceremonious, public sanction. A lot of people sanctioned my husband to take my body or leave it. They gave him the right to curl up and sleep with his back towards me when he was tired. To not take me in his arms when he did not want to. To reach out for me when he wanted. The choice was always his. To be with me, or without me. It was never mine. It was the same with Samir. He came in to my life unasked. He went away unasked. I never wanted to be owned by either of them. Or disowned. I just wanted love. I tried to love Gautam. I loved Samir. I never learnt what they loved. If they loved anything at all.'

Papu clasped my hands tight. I looked with wonder at them. They were living hands. They were not cold. Then he said, 'You are your truth. Whatever happens, whoever comes or goes or stays, you stay true to that truth. And don't be afraid.'

He laughed, 'And whenever you see "No Fear" written behind a car, remember it's a message from me!'

He hugged me. I stayed close to his chest for many moments. I closed my eyes. When I opened them, he was gone.

31

DAYS WALKED BY with wooden feet. Gautam spent a lot of time with me. He gave me a bath everyday, brought me bowls of soup and combed my hair.

One evening Sarita walked in with some roses when Gautam had gone out for a walk.

'Who is Samir?' she asked, smelling her roses deeply.

'Why do you want to know?' I put my book aside to face her.

'You were talking to two men in the hospital. One of them was Samir.' Her voice was flat except for a faint bump of curiosity.

'He is someone I know. Used to know.'

She put the roses next to me and sat down by my feet, 'Didn't seem like that to me. You were in his arms and showing him wild flowers in your hair.'

I went back to my book.

'Who is he?'

'He is gone.'

'I don't think so. You don't either. If you did, he would not have been in the hospital ward with you.'

We grew quiet.

'What was he like?' She leaned forward.

I did not answer.

'You can see him even when you can't, right? You remember his walk. The smell of him. The way he sat. The way he looked at you. His voice. His laughter. The things he said and the things he didn't. You are in love with him. Then why did you marry Gautam?'

I smiled at her, 'Because you couldn't.'

She looked away. I suddenly felt sorry for her. 'When you came into my home that night—that is all it was, wasn't it? All the pain he had put you through by not being the man you wanted him to be, you took out on me. Nothing touched me beyond a point because you were more desperate to keep him than I was.'

She remained quiet waiting for more and then said slowly, 'Two years back, I went to Chennai for my father's funeral and Gautam met me at the airport with flowers,' she smiled to herself, 'and in the taxi, told me he had missed me and asked if I wanted to marry him. I did, but the way he said it . . . it scared me. It was like he wanted to fix something, do the right thing, whatever. As if the right thing was not what we had but something outside of him. Like if he married me, he could prove to himself just how dispassionately he could take the most important decision of his life. He wanted to do the right thing by me . . . my father having passed away and all and not because we were in love. I refused and never realised that he would not ask me again, the right way, or that he would go ahead and marry someone else.'

'Sarita, I married him because when he came to sit next

to me on the couch, I felt his gentleness, his decency reach out to me and at that moment, it was enough. But it *wasn't*. After we got married I saw that he lives outside of himself, by a book of righteousness perhaps, but never on the impulse of real passion, anger or pain. You know him better than I do. Why is he like this? He is always made up as if he is playing someone else's version of him. No one can touch him, feel him, get through to him and he can't do it either. Why?'

She looked straight at me for the first time, 'I don't know, though I do know that by the time his parents separated, he had seen enough of the mess that people can make of their lives to not want the same for himself. He left Delhi to escape his past and ran right into me here. The fact that I'm older than him, drink, have dependency problems did not help. Still, he tried to make sense of me . . . But then maybe he gave up and just wanted a safe marriage where everything would be arranged and sorted by the only people he trusts. Little did he know!'

We both laughed.

Then I said, 'I have to leave and I will once I'm strong enough to walk out of that door. Believe me, this whole thing is unreal and I feel everything . . . is happening to someone else. As if I am not even here. But you are and he is, so . . .'

She shook her head. 'He feels responsible for me but I don't think he will ever come back. That time when I made him stay at my place during the riots? We almost . . . you know. But he shut himself up in the guest room. He was married enough to say no to me, but not enough to want to leave. Then you went to pieces and you should have seen him. He was just so surprised that things could go wrong so fast, to that extent, and you know, it is hard for him to understand why you did it. He can't believe that anyone can react so strongly to anything. Especially, because he always does the right thing—in his mind atleast.'

'He never asked me why I did it. Not even once.'

'I did something I'm not very proud of . . . among other things. I wrote a letter to your mother. I took the address from him and told him that I was going to break the news to her, being a mutual friend, and he did not stop me. I . . . I told her that she should come and look after you and take charge because he was not able to.'

I shrugged, 'I was going to write to her, anyway. Maybe she would have tried to reason with me, but because you wrote the letter, she will have to face the facts.'

Once back at home from the hospital, I gave Gautam no reason to believe that our marriage was spent. I waited for Ma and quietly went back to my job and packing my things whenever I had some time to myself.

It was a Sunday morning when he noticed my packed suitcases in the store room.

'What are those?' he asked.

'My bags.'

He stood indecisively for a moment and then went to the living room to continue watching his favourite comedy show on TV and finish his tuna sandwich. Something had died in the house. I could smell it even though I knew I would never find what it was.

Ma arrived that evening with just one bag. Gautam served her tea and biscuits. We all sat watching the smoke curl above our tea cups.

'You should have told me earlier,' Ma said to me. Gautam kept his eyes on the smoke curls.

'I don't see why Sarita had to write to me. You should have had the guts to end this marriage. I didn't give you to Sarita. I gave you to Gautam and both of you should not have needed another person to speak on your behalf. Sarita wrote that I should come and take charge of the situation. What is this situation, if I may ask?'

I had never heard Ma using such a forcefully decisive tone and I said, 'The fact is Ma, this really is no marriage because . . . it just isn't . . . and I don't want to spend the next ten years of my life discovering that every day.'

The smoke curls were gone and the mismatched tea cups lay forgotten on the centre table. I noticed the greasy, old circles left on the pinewood grains by wet cups and wondered how they would come off. Then I realised I did not have to worry about it.

Gautam's eyes were glazed with panic and fear. He seemed desperate, like a man who is too far away to board a train that is beginning to shudder and is left behind with nowhere to go.

'Mummyji, Sarita is just a friend. That's all. I am never going to end this marriage. I am never going to file for divorce or anything. I am totally committed. Sarita was just worried about another suicide attempt and we didn't of course know what had triggered it the first time. I didn't know what to say to you so Sarita wrote. But I realise, it was a mistake. I will take care from now on.'

I asked him, 'You discussed this with her but not with me? You never asked me why I did it. Why?'

He laced his fingers together and cleared his throat, 'I did not know how to. I was scared.'

'Of what? That I would blame you? I don't. I just fell apart because I can deal with anything if it is real and resonates with me, but this was false, right from the hair they pinned on my head during the wedding. You hear everything I say Gautam, but you don't listen. You cannot understand why I want more than what you can give me. But I do want more. And I can't spend my life in denial.'

Ma asked him, 'Are you happy?'

He nodded back, 'Yes.'

Ma swayed her head, 'Really? You can't even face what you really feel. How will you deal with what she feels? I have no doubt that you mean well. But it is not enough. For you or her.'

Gautam arranged for two flight tickets for Ma and me. At the airport, his body was leaden with misery. His hands reached out for mine. I remembered them on my body.

Then I told him, 'Take care.'

'You too. And you can always send for a return ticket,' he said.

'I won't,' I smiled.

32

ON THE PLANE, Ma told me about Samir's wedding.

'The girl is someone he met at one of Anna's parties. They've been together for some time and the wedding will take place in two months. I saw him sometime back and he looks as wonderful as ever, but seems to have nothing to say to anyone, anymore,' Ma looked at me. I looked away, to concentrate on Alaskan lakes and cloudy bears floating past my window.

The same evening, as our bus hurtled from Delhi towards Patiala, I looked out from my rusty, grilled window to drink in the familiarity of the world I had left behind. When the sugarcane fields of Punjab appeared and yellow mustard flowers nodded at the bus, something began to move in my throat and to sting my eyes. Bahadurgarh's old fort glinted in the setting sun and Punjabi University whizzed past in a haze of white and blue. When the bus stopped, I remembered what a Patialawi shop-keeper had once told me, 'Guddi . . . you may go and strike your roots anywhere but Patiala will always call you back again and again. The water here is such. Once you drink it, you can't forget it. You will thirst for it everywhere.'

I reached home to discover that Ma had befriended her empty house. It was her second skin now. It had aged on her bones softly and settled in pulpy, creamy folds around her. It had supplanted Papu in her heart. She had agonised over every new sign of age on its walls and laboured to patch it, white-wash it, heal it. The house now held no secrets from her. She entered the cemented water-tank at least once a month, with her salwar rolled up, to scrub and clean it of grime. She knew by heart, the contours of every rough patch on the cemented floor of the drawing room where Papu's printing press had once stood. I re-learnt Ma's non-negotiable house rules: the stapler, the glue-tube and the scissors stayed in the left side-table; the envelopes, stamps, parcel wax, candles and matchboxes, in the right one. The plump red sofa had to be dusted and wiped with a damp cloth everyday. The jute owl on the wall behind the TV had to be shaken and his blackberry nose wiped clean of dust.

Every Sunday, jars and masala bottles had to be taken down from their grooves and kitchen shelves had to be lined with fresh newspapers. And when the house was wrapped up in the aroma of its own health, Ma sat on the dining table with a glass of tea and a rusk and sipped contentment slowly.

She told me she had been tempted to sell the home to a young family. 'Anna wanted me to settle in Ambrosa,' she said. But she could not leave Patiala because she could not see No 7, Bakshi Ganda Singh Street inhabited by history wipers of any kind. She could not bear to imagine strange vessels in her kitchen. Or someone else's clothes in the cement alcoves Papu had designed for her.

This was the only home she had ever had. The only home she had ever owned. It was a monument to wistfulness and a reminder of all that Ma did not have. Yet, she had never felt at home anywhere else.

The home town, I realised, is a memory of smells that trigger off unbearable nostalgia and unbearable joy, a place too small in retrospect but also the incubator of dreams, a womb of safety, a well-thumbed album of mohallas, familiar faces that smile at you, little lanes you will never be lost in, small shops with fading signboards and beloved bazaars fraying at the edges.

Patiala had changed a little in my absence. A flyover was being built near the bus stand. The bazaars looked narrower than I remembered. A new Sheranwala Gate was in construction. My colonial school building now hosted an officer's training institute. The school had been shifted elsewhere. Mall Road's glorious landmarks, Phul and Malwa, were there too, though there were rumours that huge, glass-fronted malls would replace them soon.

After a few weeks had passed and we had spent all that needed to be said about my marriage and how it had petered off, Ma told me of an angry letter she had received from Delhi, accusing me of wrecking the marriage and how Nimmo aunty had always believed I was not marriage material and very far from the kind of woman Gautam should have married.

Ma shuddered, 'She is very upset with the fact that you have no respect for the "sacred Indian traditions" and the institution of marriage which women must uphold no matter what or society will go to pieces!'

I laughed, 'She should have seen Sarita then; maybe she will, who knows?'

'You don't care if Gautam divorces you and marries her?' Ma looked curious even though she knew the answer. When I shrugged, she said, 'I went to Ambrosa some time back. It is still a happy place but there will be no tea aristocrats in Annaville after Inder. He's too tired to manage the estate alone and Anna finally asked Samir to come back home.'

Samir had come back but not to feed his life to the tea gardens. He had told Inder uncle that he would stay only if he was allowed to use parts of the estate to build a resort. Samir told him that Ambrosa's tea was dying. That it could not compete with the cheaper tea imports. Ma swayed her head with gentle disapproval, 'He told Inder that, to survive, tea needs to be demystified. He is building about twenty cottages at the centre of the estate. There is also a tea boutique or something. A few acres of tea will stay, but Inder is not very happy. He feels violated. He cannot understand Samir's irreverence for something he has spent his life nurturing. But then we are all growing old. And Annaville is older than both Anna and Inder. All three of them need Samir. They have spent enough time away from him.'

She looked at me then and said, 'Anna wants to meet you.'

When I boarded the train to Asankot a few days later, Ma told me, 'I wanted to you to go alone this time. If there is anything unresolved, sort it out. Samir is getting married. Try not to forget that.'

I nodded, 'Annaville was safe from me even when he was on his own. I am going there for myself. Not for him.'

33

I STARTED FROM Patiala on a cold, purple evening. Asankot did not look any different from the train but Ambrosa was no longer the green, lush valley of my dreams. Winter had shocked its pine slopes into a brown silence and the mountains looked like hairy camel humps—Harigiri, the starkest of them all. The sky was a blinding blue and water springs once swollen by melting summer snows had vanished. Gnarled tree colonies looked older and their knotty vines looked bruised and naked without leaves. A haze of quarry dust hung over the skeletal Chawli.

Brash new restaurants had bitten into mountains. Knolls gaped with deep mouthfuls of garbage. Everywhere I turned, I saw public menus, public toilets and election agendas, all co-existing on mutilated mountain sides. Flat-roofed housing colonies had finished off the tea gardens that Samir and I had once streamed past on his bike. Even Annaville's gate looked different under its fresh, wet coat of paint.

But Anna aunty was still there, standing on the veranda steps, waiting to welcome me, like always. That had not changed. Nor had her fragrance. But she looked smaller, and browner, then my memories of her. Her eyes looked larger too, as if they could not believe the world changing around her. The perfect bones of her face were still sharp, but there was a mellowness to them. As if they were filled with a sweet nectar and would dissolve soon.

It had not been that long. Just about four years since I had seen her last, but maybe time had turned more wilful, less forgiving to all things beautiful.

Inder uncle gave me a hug too, and I noticed the fresh snow at his temples. The first thing I saw inside was the photograph on the mantelpiece. It had Samir and her. They were posing against the same mantelpiece, smiling into the camera. And there were some new things. Little Swiss huts, prints of paintings by American artists. Little milestones of Samir's journey through the world.

Anna aunty took me to the kitchen and talked to me as she supervised lunch. Bala had died the previous year and the new boy was fumbling with the stuffed tomatoes. 'Pin the lids with a toothpick,' she told him gently and turned to me. 'Samir's cottages will be ready for tourists within a month and you should see him. He looks like a ghost. He really is taking too much on himself and hardly spends any time with Navya.'

'Navya?' I asked.

'His fiancée. She is a family friend's niece and was visiting from the US and they ran into each other at one of our house parties. I don't know if any sparks flew, but something must have happened for him to make such a big commitment . . .' Anna aunty looked puzzled as she tried to put her together. 'She is fair, slim—fashionably so—and looks good in everything girls wear these days. And has a good telephone voice, if that counts. That's about all I can tell you about her. We wanted the family priest to give us an auspicious date for the wedding, but you know Samir. No one can ever give him anything he doesn't want. He will marry her when he is ready.'

When Samir walked in, I was grateful for the cold in my veins. For the heart that was now cotton-woolled against him.

'Hi,' he smiled.

'Hi,' I said and extended my hand, 'and congratulations.'

'For what?' he took my hand.

'On your engagement,' I said, looking him squarely in the eye.

I took care not to see anything else. Not him at all. Just his eyes. As if they were not his at all, but of a man I did not know.

'Oh . . . I thought you were talking about the resort. You want to come? Stay there for a couple of days? I need help with the interiors,' he said.

My hand was still in his. I took it back and said, 'Sure. But only for a few days. I'm here to spend time with Anna aunty.'

'I didn't think otherwise,' he said grimly, struggling to make his slow smile as impersonal as his anger, and walked away.

Anna aunty looked at me, 'Are you two still at it? God, I used to feel like a circus master with a whip during those summers. But knowing what I know of you two . . . why couldn't you get along? This is one mystery I haven't been able to solve. I asked Samir many times. He just shrugged.

You got along so well as kids. Then something happened in your teens, didn't it? I thought maybe your hormones were fighting and once they settled down you would too. But no. You still can't talk to each other without swords and body armours.'

'We are fine,' I told her.

After lunch, Inder uncle went to his study. Anna aunty and I settled in the veranda, drinking the pine-apple wine Samir had made for the resort.

Samir joined us but stretched out on a distant chair, studiously looking away from us. His glass glimmered like a yellow diamond in the sunlight.

'Can I ask you about Gautam?' Anna aunty asked me under her breath. I saw Samir turn towards us and look straight at me. His hands were suddenly stiff around his glass.

'Nothing to tell, really,' I said. 'He is very gentle. He doesn't believe in hurting anyone. In all the time I was with him, he never raised his voice once at me or slammed a door in my face. He never said anything he didn't mean and meant everything he said.' Samir turned his face away. I continued, 'But he had nothing to say to me. Being married to him was like being alone. That was all.'

Anna aunty nodded.

'Are you ready? Your luggage is already in the car,' Samir called out as he rose.

'Yes,' I said.

Tek Singh, now much thinner and whiter, smiled at me and opened the door of a prosperous, new car. Samir took the seat next to the driver and I settled in the back seat.

I tried not too breathe too deeply. I did not want to smell

Samir's aftershave. The car began to glide. Noticing that we both were quiet, Tek Singh slipped in a cassette of Punjabi folk songs. '*Doli chadke Heer ne bain kiye,*' he sang softly. I remembered the poet Waris Shah's Heer who had died for the love of her Ranjha. I wanted to laugh. No one even cared about living for love anymore. Who would die for it?

'Why did you come back?' I asked Samir.

He turned back and smiled, 'No special reason if you discount Ma. I had a good time, but I learnt one thing. After a while it does not really matter if you find a pot of shit or a pot of gold at the end of a rainbow. Both smell the same.' Then he laughed and turned away, 'Well . . . maybe not. Fact is . . . I don't have roots anywhere. I can settle down anywhere and still feel unsettled. So doesn't matter where I am. I don't really feel at home anywhere.'

We were swerving around a green-haired bend when another car appeared opposite and froze in its tracks. It silently fumed. As if to say that, if it wasn't allowed to pass first, no one would reach anywhere in time.

Tek Singh switched off the music and waited. The windshield of the other car looked blankly at him. Not budging. Then a head appeared from it. And a voice broke against our windshield, 'Oye Khoteya, you bring this turban from Punjab and you think you can tell a local driver to give you way? Move away you bastard or I will force this steel whore of yours off the road!'

'Stay inside,' Samir told me as he opened the door and sprang out. But Tek Singh was out before him. 'No, let me tackle this,' he restrained Samir with a steady hand. He walked up to the car and knocked on the windshield. The door swung open.

A short, stocky man swaying under a traditional Kangra cap stepped out and barked, 'What you dungur? You want to make Khalistan in Ambrosa too? Are you Bhinderwale's son that I should let you pass first? We don't allow terrorists or their sons on our land.'

'How long have you been in Ambrosa?' the old Sikh asked him.

'Why? What is it to you?' asked the man leaning towards him.

'I have been here since the last fifty-six years. This boy you see next to me has the blood of four generations of tea planters in his veins. I don't have an estate like him here but my ancestors came to Ambrosa even before his ancestors. Our mitti is everywhere. And our blood, our sweat, our tears. And you drunken dog, stand there telling me that I don't belong here because I wasn't born wearing a Kangra cap? Yes, I brought my turban from Punjab but where did you bring that tongue from? It is not the tongue of a man born and brought up in Ambrosa. It is not the tongue of my people or my home town. And now if you want to take your cap and your head and your tongue back home safely, you will move your vehicle out of the way. Or saabji here and I will help you do it.'

The man looked at him and then at Samir and then walked back to his car. Within five minutes, Heer was once again mourning the loss of love in our whooshing car and Tek Singh was singing along with her.

'That is our tea factory,' Samir pointed to his left. I saw a huge, black-windowed, brown-bricked building. Its insides looked empty even from outside. I looked away. The sun had almost dipped below the edges of the mountains. When the car swung in the middle of an orange-tinged sea of tea-leaves, I wondered why I had never seen this side of Samir. His tea gardens. His factory which was once a young, bustling place but now dying slowly. Perhaps because Samir himself had never claimed all of this as his own. Once upon a time, these gardens had been orchestrated with great flourish by Inder uncle's ancestors. The tea had been a celebration of their blood-deep arrogance. It had been as rejuvenating as pine breath.

Inder uncle had inherited his father's passion for his Harigiri-flavoured mellow acres. Like a family heirloom, he had passed them on to Samir. But it was a futile gift and it would lie unopened. Because Samir never wanted anything that was given to him. Like all the other gifts, this one too would gather dust and cobwebs in some dark, unlit, unvisited place in his life.

The car bruised the edges of tea-gardens and I smelt their China-hybrid grief as they watched Samir go by. I heard myself say, 'I have never been here. But this is so beautiful. I can't understand why it has to die . . .'

Samir turned to look at me, 'Long before Papa was born, our tea sold well at auctions in Amritsar. People in Kashmir and even Afghanistan drank it. Now we won't be able to sell it even in the next town if we wanted.'

He smiled, 'As things grow, they mutate. We are all born with all the pieces of our personal jigsaw puzzles but then we misplace the pieces. Everything gets scattered. Everything is divided. People, neighbourhoods, nations, idealism. Where is the place for a man like Papa anywhere in the world now? He still believes he can keep his world safe from breaking up into pieces. He is wrong. I tell him he should join politics. At least that way he will be able to do something for this place. Otherwise, people who have no love for this place will come with alien manifestos and divide us for votes. The man you just saw is an exception now. In the future, he may rule all of us.'

Heer had stopped singing and Tek Singh was quiet too. The tea gardens began to slope away and led the car to a scraped, wooden plank. Its torched letters said, 'Ambrosia'. 'Ma thought of the name and she is very pleased with herself,' Samir laughed.

We got out of the car and the gravel under my feet turned noisy. Samir held out a hand to help me climb a broad, steep flight of quarry stone stairs. He withdrew it when I climbed on without looking at him. His voice was a little strained when he said, 'The site was rather uneven so we left it untouched. I got an architect friend from Delhi to build cottages without levelling the slopes.'

The cottages were part wood, part stone and topped with slate. 'The plants all came from Annaville,' Samir pointed at the raging creepers crawling up the walls and the roofs.

We walked to a cottage through a bougainvillea arch, a frenzied patch of wild flowers, and climbed into a veranda with two pinewood chairs. Samir opened the door of the cottage and looked at me. His gaze was tight with excitement. 'This is it,' he said, letting me pass first.

I saw an exposed stone wall with a hollow, dark-mouthed fireplace. Roughly plastered white walls. A pinewood floor. And oceans of green tea lapping against all the windows. There were window seats and rough pinewood couches stuffed with fruity, citrus cushions.

'Nice,' I said.

'You must be tired. I will show you the rest of the place later. See that?' He opened a window and pointed at a glass-walled structure.

'That is the highest level of the property. It is a restaurant and club. It has a bar, a snooker table, a TV set, music system, a small library and table tennis. And that is the pool,' he said, pointing to a distant cobalt shimmer.

When Samir left, I took a long breath. Relieved that I no longer needed to hold my breath.

I picked up the welcome note in a fruit and chocolate basket and recognised the handwriting. And remembered the letters that had once slipped into my letter-box like forbidden hopes.

Just as I was finishing unpacking, I heard panic-stricken feet and the smell of fire that Ma had bred in my bones. I ran out and saw Samir standing at the foot of a pine mountain, shouting instructions to a group of people with fire extinguishers. The mountain was dark save a glowing serpent that hissed angrily and spit out little flames. He was shouting, 'The next time I catch someone smoking in this property, I will personally skin them alive.'

Then he turned to look at me, 'These mountains turn into hay stacks this time of the year and just one matchstick can start a fire, but who will explain this to these idiots? The launch is just a month away and if even one tourist smells smoke behind his cottage, he will take the next flight home and tell his neighbours how unsafe Indian hotels are. Anyway, freshen up and get ready. I am expecting a lot of my personal guests today and they will be here soon.'

Later, while undressing in the bathroom, I smiled at the way the roof sloped down at me with its glass tile insets and the rough stone and plastered walls felt like loaves of multi-grain bread. I ran my heels over river pebbles embedded in the flooring. I had finished dressing when I heard the tap on the door.

Samir stood outside, leaning against a stone pillar, in a crsip white shirt and dark trousers. His eyes ran over me. The tanned linen of the long dress Gautam had bought me once. My jute slippers. There was a half-smile around his mouth. I knew I could no longer escape looking at him. So I allowed myself to notice that he looked darker. That his eyes were a deeper shade of caramel now. That his smile was quieter and so was his gaze. He walked in and stood next to a large window. His eyes checked the room for a wrong note and then stopped at me, 'You like this?'

'It's brave,' I answered and added, 'and quite unnecessary. But then, maybe, you always do what you don't need to.'

He threw his head back and laughed, 'I prefer my carrots without a pinch of salt. But thanks anyway. And remember one thing. Cynicism is the most useless emotion in the world. It kills things even before they are dead.'

He had touched a wound and I winced.

He waited for me to say something and then said, 'I need help with this. I want the cottages to come alive. To speak to the visitors. I hate clutter but drama is fine. Do what you want. Take your time.'

'You need nothing here except Annaville. Old pictures. Ripe wheat stalks. Antique urns. Flowers. Cane baskets. Stoneware. Masks and Tibetan rugs.'

He smiled, 'You are different now, you know?'

'Different how?' I asked.

'Somehow. You look . . . deeper. I'm different too. I did

miss my vocation of being an usher at your art shows, but I can hire you as my in-house designer. If you don't mind.'

'I don't,' I smiled.

We waited for more words.

Then I told him, 'I'm glad all your dreams came true.'

He smiled and shrugged, 'Sometimes I just want my youth back. When I was still dreaming. I just want some time now. To dream.'

I held his gaze and said, 'I don't remember you ever dreaming. You always wanted to live the life you are leading now. Anna aunty always told me that life gives us what we ask of it. And you have everything that you asked for.'

He listened intently, as if trying to understand more than what was being said. Then he said, 'I wish life always gave us what we asked of it, but it has a mind of its own. A lot of things happened in my life that I didn't plan. I am not as cold-blooded as you think I am . . . it wasn't easy to walk away from a lot of things. But I had to. It hurt. But then one picks up the strands and moves on.'

He studied my silence for a moment before continuing, 'Before I came here, I was trekking through south-eastern parts of British Columbia. I lost track of time and reached a mountain cliff very late at night. I just sat there and heard the breeze blowing all around me. I felt there was no living thing between the earth and the sky except me. And then I thought . . .'

He looked away, leaving the sentence unfinished. I asked, 'And then you thought what?'

His eyes came back to my face and he said, 'I can't remember now but I am sure whatever it was, it was very interesting.'

He began to walk away, 'Anytime you need something, just ask for me. You decide what you want to do with each room. Don't work too hard though. I want you to enjoy your stay here.'

After he left, the laughter of dinner-hungry guests filled up the restaurant and I walked towards them to meet Samir's future.

Anna aunty and Inder uncle sat surrounded by old friends, and Samir, slender in a black jacket, walked around, checking the buffet platters simmering over the food warmers and talking to the waiters.

I settled down next to Anna aunty and sipped something. She said, 'I can see he is ready for marriage but . . . I don't know. That's her.'

Then I saw Samir lean over a woman and kiss the top of her head.

Till now all the women Samir had loved had been phantoms. I had never seen any of them, but I had grown up resenting strange, warm, brandy voices on Annaville's phone lines. I had grown up fearing Samir's photo albums and the indelible faces plastered in them. There had been so much to fear. The clock in his room—gifted to him by a girlfriend. The Old Spice silk shirts he wore before a date.

I could never see a beautiful girl without a jab of resentment. I always wondered what Samir would do if he ever saw her. If he would smile a slow smile and lope towards her to talk. I knew what he liked in a woman because I had never been that woman.

His woman would laugh and frown in the right proportion and speak with wit but no emotion. She would be groomed to perfection and never have any inner or outer split ends.

Glinting teeth, bleached arms, a bright and even accent and soft curves and hard planes. Good breeding worn like a pretty nail polish and detached passion. And a mind that would never think of Samir as life or death.

And this then was the woman in whom Samir had found all this and more. She was talking to someone. No spotlight burnt above her head. This was no phantom woman of my imagination. Her hair did not fall like the night around her—it was cut in a neat, school-girl bob. Her cheekbones did not look down at anyone with insolence. She had the yielding mouth and adoring eyes of a baby. I looked away and watched the paper lanterns and hurricane lamps instead.

34

SUDDENLY SOMEONE MENTIONED Ayodhya. And
then even the breeze grew quiet. We could hear the food
bubble softly.

'I have audio cassettes of speeches,' an old acquaintance
of Inder uncle's said.

I had seen him occasionally at Annaville. Talking, drinking,
eating too loudly. Making Anna aunty go 'Ssssss' in the
kitchen. I heard that sound in her face now, in the faint
crease between her smooth brows.

'I have cassettes,' he slurped over an imaginary meat
chunk and tapped his gin glass with an overgrown nail. He
surveyed his audience as if it were made of indeterminate
heads and shoulders and he was watching them from a
white-lit, oversized stage. He relished each word, squeezing
its contours into a pulp, 'You should hear. These people
know something. Some politicians at least talk sense. Their
speeches made me proud to be a Hindu. Why should we
apologise for who we are? We have been patient far too
long. The minorities should behave like minorities. This is

not their land. It is ours. The mosque had to go. The temple has to be built in the land of Rama. . . .'

Then I heard myself. And Papu, 'What do you mean when you say a minority?'

The man sought for a face in the mass of darkness spread before him. Then his eyes settled on me disbelievingly, 'Oh, it's you! How are you beti? Last time I saw you, you were in a frock. How are you? You got married, didn't you? Mrs Inder told me. Where is your husband?'

'What is a minority?'

'Hmm,' his eye-balls rolled from the cornea of one eye to another. His head tilted to one side to weigh the question. 'You know what I mean. People who don't belong here.'

'Do you think I do?' I asked him.

'You? Of course. You are one of us. You are a Hindu, aren't you? All Hindus are one family.'

'But my mother was not born in your India—she was born in what you now call Pakistan. The majority in Pakistan one day claimed her country as her own, killed her parents and threw her at what remained of India. But she could never be a part of your majority because she wasn't born here. My father too would have been a refugee in his own home if terrorism had survived in Punjab. He too would have been asked to leave even though he was born a Punjabi. Even though he lived as a Punjabi and died as one, wearing a Sikh kada on his wrist.

'And me? His daughter? According to your mathematics, I don't belong anywhere either. I was a minority Hindu in Punjab. A minority Punjabi in Bangalore which incidentally is full of minority Muslims, Christians, Tamilians, Malayalis, Biharis. To make things worse, I am a woman and women are in a minority everywhere. Today I saw a lout calling Inder uncle's Sikh driver an outsider. If he finds out you were not born in Ambrosa, he will want to call you names too. We are all outsiders and we are all in a minority when we step outside our homes. And we are all at risk because the law of the majority will some day catch up with all of us. Including you. Then where will you run? Where will you go when you find that you too are in the minority of one?'

It was only when I felt wet grass and harsh gravel under my heels that I realised that I had left behind the silence at the table, smoking along with the food, and was walking alone between the tea bushes. The pathway was like the rage inside me. Bleached white under the dripping halogen lights and twisted into a rope that I held with both my hands and whipped myself with.

Why had I come back to Ambrosa? I was never meant to be a part of it. Or to belong here. Or grow old here. Like Tek Singh, I too did not belong. I was the branded outsider. A daughter without an inheritance. Without a tea estate to reject. Born to a mother whose soul was cut in half. Born in a brave home with blotchy walls and a scarred cement floor. From a womb that had fed me grief and memories of every stab-wound time had given Ma because there had been nothing else to remember. Nothing else except Samir. Except that he had been the biggest stab wound of all. The only link with a future that could never be.

He had just been a curious onlooker leaning out of a yellow-lit window, watching me amusedly as I passed by. I wasn't someone he would ever open the door for. He had just been a straw fluttering out from my dreams into the real world and yet I had clung to him to swim through my life.

I had walked around Perfect Eight's silken loops forever to reach Samir and Annaville and I was still lost, as was Ma. So were all those who were marked by history to always be divided from the rest of the world in irreconcilable halves and lived with too little faith and too much fear.

My legs began to ache.

When I got back to my cottage, my balcony was yellow in the night and Samir was waiting on a chair. His legs resting on another. With eyes that looked tired and heavy with the deferred sleep of many nights.

35

'YOU CAN'T GO very far on a monologue and empty stomach, can you? Since when did you start thinking about all this? And I thought I knew everything there was to know about you. Now go inside and eat your soup before it gets cold. I took the liberty of calling up room-service and ordering some for you,' he said.

His jacket was around his shoulders and the tie was off. 'And it is not safe to walk alone so late. This place is famous for ghosts. Though you will never catch me mentioning that in the hotel brochure!' he joked.

We laughed half-heartedly and then silence fell around us again.

'Alright then,' he swung his legs to get up. It was the same as always. Nothing had changed. He would go. And I would stay.

I shut the door loudly behind him. I was pouring myself a glass of water when I heard his knock. I opened the door and he walked in.

When the world was left outside on the footmat, he looked at me.

He watched me through a frown. Then he spoke, 'You remember that peach jam Ma used to make? It was my favourite, but I never ate too much of it. It was enough that it was there. I never craved it because I knew it was there on that window sill, waiting to be opened. I don't know why I should think of that now.

'Anyway, I never missed you all these years. Not for a moment. When I closed my eyes, I could not even remember your face. Except once when I saw you in a dream. I saw this house with white walls. Blue curtains. And I went from room to room looking for you. I finally found you, sitting on a squarish, large bed, wearing a yellow dress, reading Ghalib. I walked up to you and your face came alive. I don't remember what we said to each other but I lifted you up like a child. Up in the air and then I embraced you. But once the dream broke, you ceased to matter. You meant nothing. Nothing, do you understand?'

I understood. Even what he hadn't said. I knew that one morning, perhaps when he was brushing his teeth and thinking of nothing, his life had run out. The joy in it, it had run out, and he didn't even know.

He smiled, 'When I saw you in Ma's kitchen today, I remembered that dream. And your face in it. Funny, how the mind plays tricks on us ... You have never been real, you know. Just a memory. No, not even that. Just a ghost, the memory of a memory. Just a faceless little monkey in a cheap satin frock with cheap plastic flowers. Small, brown and tousled. Stinking like a rag-doll. Watching me. Shivering with hate at my touch. Running away. Crawling back, always crawling back ...'

Samir shook his head, 'Something happened on that

goddamned night in that goddamned bed even though what happened between us was nothing. Almost as insignificant as this one flaring matchstick which started the mountain fire you just saw. It was just a moment when I felt you next to me and wanted nothing more than to somehow make you mine. You did not resist and then suddenly, I felt your loathing. Your breath and your clothes reeked of it and we were never the same people after that. Do you think you alone got hurt by what we started? Do you think I felt nothing when you ran away? You ran away. From me! It wasn't something I could forgive.'

He walked to the door and turned around, 'We were never children. You and I. We always had old, greedy, unforgiving souls. I knew even then that one day I would have you at my feet. Begging to be loved. And you did come. But you didn't beg. You spat love at me like an insult. And then you left. I didn't know then that you would take my life away with you. But you knew it, didn't you? How the hell did you know that? Who taught you to love like that? I tried to sort out this thing between us. Many times. But you . . .'

His eyes narrowed with hate, 'You want more than this hunger that we have for each other. Whatever it is, you are not going to get it. I am not going to bleed at your feet. But there's something only you can tell me. Why do I still feel you like a knife in a wound? Why can't I forget? Why does it still hurt when you walk away like you did tonight?'

There was just the hush of pines between us and then he lifted his head, his eyes full of me and said, 'Ira.'

I heard my name as if he had spoken it for the first time. Maybe he had.

'Why?' he asked.

'Because Samir,' I said, 'it was love. And because you walked away.'

He walked back to me. I heard him breathe. Slowly. As if he was trying not to.

He stopped within inches of me. I felt his hands first on my wrists, cupping them, cutting off the pain running through my blood.

Then his palms opened to slide up my arms and to quieten them. His hands stilled the night when they reached my shoulders. They stayed there, without committing anything.

I stepped closer and clasped him with a long, feather-soft moment. Just my arms around his neck and my head resting on his chest. Our bodies barely touching. It was the simplest thing I had ever done.

His hands slowly rose to my neck. Warm, slim hands that made pine-apple wine and pinned perfect bowties on crisp, white shirts. Hands that had once touched me against my will. Written guarded letters to me. Played chess. Held rebellious cigarettes, steering wheels and other women.

These hands were mine now and I was theirs. They held my face and lifted it.

I saw the eyes that had looked at me so many times, only to look away.

I felt them now like a hungry flame on my face, on my mouth. I saw the fine stubble on Samir's chin, the smooth rectangle of his forehead where the sun rose every morning.

His tousled hair. The small ears. The mouth that never had to ask for anything.

He closed his eyes and took a sharp breath when I

touched the bridge of his nose. The line of his jaw. The nape of his neck. Then he pulled me close and turned himself over to me. To feel all of him. His body and its long, flowing lines. His chest. His arms. His hips. His thighs. His tight, tense, bruising bones. His hungry, bristling blood. The sum of all his past lives. All his hurts, joys, sorrows, triumphs. His darkness and his light. The taste of his sweat. The dark rum on his tongue. The bite of musk in his armpits.

Then his face came closer and closer till his mouth blurred in mine. When I bit him back, he broke free and laughed. And lifted me. Before my feet touched the ground, he caught my lips again.

This is my body, I told myself in wonder. My body in Samir's hands. His in mine. My mouth on his. His on mine. Drinking from it. Feeding it. Feeding on it. His hands on my back, hurting my ribs, discovering my breasts. And his legs pressing into mine with blind hunger. His hunger that had taught me a long time back to hunger for him. To ache for him like a wound. An aching, gaping and yawning wound.

I had pulled that hunger out of my memory and thrown it away. But it had survived everything, and crawled back into my life on its bloody belly. How had I lived so many lives carrying this wound? How had I lived without knowing what it was to touch Samir and to be touched by Samir?

Samir knew my body as if it were his. He touched it without deference. Without fear. Without doubt. Our hunger for each other was so old. Older perhaps even than the pine mountains of Ambrosa and the sugar cane fields of a Punjabi farmhouse where he and I had first touched each other.

He broke away for an instant to breathe and then we were on a cool bed, pinched and patted only a few hours ago in neat planes by Samir's staff, now a little island of tumult in a sea of liquid moon and soft, silver shadows.

Samir's eyes were half-closed and his mouth full with a smile I had never forgotten.

Before he cut off my breath again, he whispered, 'Don't frown. Smile at me. Try it.'

When I shook my head, he laughed and pressed me back into the moonlit pillows and blocked the rest of the world with his shoulders. Then there was nothing between us except the pine breeze, the night, his scalding breath and his slow-burning skin.

We drank from each other. My hands branding his skull, twisting the roots of his hair. His arms around me, his hands and his mouth seeking me, shredding my body and my soul into long flame ribbons.

I did not remember what I had worn in the evening. I knew only that Samir had ripped it off me and I did not need to hide myself from him anymore. And that he was gleaming in the night. And that I had waited long enough.

When he found me with an impatient groan, I clung to him with all the years I had spent away from him. And with all my limbs.

With each gasp that escaped his lean, straining body, I let myself remember. Samir getting off a train in brown corduroys. Samir buying peaches from a roadside pile. Samir calling a girl on the phone, his hand drumming a chest of drawers, his eyes on me. Samir in badminton whites. Samir opening his arms to say, 'Darling'. Samir standing on the terrace, watching me though curls of cigarette smoke. Samir in a jacket, looking at me across the span of many years. Many lifetimes maybe. And Samir. And more of him. And then some more. And then more. And then the longing for him was gone because I had found him. And had arched to claim him and to keep him forever.

And then he claimed me too and with a long, shuddering moan, collapsed in my arms. His seed within me. On me. On him. And I watched the hair and the moonlight tangled in it.

When we grew cold, he pulled up the duvet to cover us both. His warmth, his breath, his smell held me with many arms. Buoyed me up from tides of pain, cradled me, embalmed all the stab wounds he had ever given me. When I moved, he groaned, 'No' and gathered me greedily to him.

He kissed my hair, my ear and whispered, 'Darling.' I rubbed my hand against his arm, smelled his chest, kissed his throat. We were quiet for a long time. Then he said, 'I didn't tell you about another dream I had a few months back. I saw you walking towards Annaville. I waited for you near the stairs but you lost your way. Then I felt someone come and stand behind me in the veranda. I turned and my blood turned to ice because it was your father. And I knew even in the dream that he . . . he was no more. He said, "Don't be afraid". And then he just stood quietly and watched me with a smile. Then he was gone. I don't know what it meant. And if it meant anything at all.'

'Maybe he wanted you to find me,' I said.

'Maybe. Go to sleep,' he whispered into my hair.

36

I WOKE UP when Samir began to move next to me. It wasn't yet dawn.

When I opened my eyes, he was walking around the room, looking for his clothes. I sat up against a pillow, watching him. He began to dress. 'I have to go,' he whispered to my shadow and left. I heard the slow creak of the door and the sound of his footsteps fading away into the darkness. The bed sheet smelt of Samir. I smelt of him too. I tried to sleep . . . wrapped up in his smell. With the aftertaste of the night in my mouth. The knowledge of having held him and being held by him had changed everything. There was nothing anymore to know, or want. We had touched despite the pain we had caused each other. Despite ourselves. Because there never had been anything or anyone else between us.

My body was spent of cold misery. It was a rainbow. A dew drop. An air bubble. It would now float away with the breeze. Nothing mattered now. Nothing could frighten me. Not even the slowly creeping dread that Samir had rid himself of the monkey on his back. And that he would never need me now.

I woke up late. The afternoon was gleaming yellow when I walked into the restaurant. The TV was on. 'I never thought, they would actually do this. Why do they have to show it, again and again. Once was enough,' I heard Tek Singh's voice among the waiters who were looking at the TV screen with the immobility of ice-sculptures.

'They look like giant ants on a piece of sugar,' the old Sikh nodded at me. Then I saw them too. The recorded footage of a majority of ants crawling all over a mosque dome in Ayodhya with pick-axes and hate-steeped weapons.

I ate a light lunch and walked around the property. Only half-registering the rooms, the pathways, new saplings, old trees.

I sat down on a deckchair near the pool and began to sketch. When I looked up, the sky had turned a dark blue. Somewhere in the property, Samir was talking aloud to someone, 'Navya loves trekking through Europe and has asked me to find her some lavender fields. She loves flowers, but for our honeymoon, I would any day opt for the Canadian hotsprings. It's quite romantic out there. They have these cosy, woody suites with attached hot springs. I can just see myself soaking in a mug of beer while the poor thing unpacks! She is a cleaning fiend. Always busy cleaning up the mess I make . . .'

His laughter had the forced glitter of fake crystal and it broke like cheap glass all around me. The pool shivered faintly, tickled by the breeze. I knew even though I didn't look up that Samir was walking towards me. When I looked up, he was standing before me. He nodded through a frown and a half-smile. His eyes looked sated. Hungry. Naked. Veiled. Curious. All-knowing.

I suddenly wondered whether all his life he had hungered for me or just for himself in my eyes. If I had ever been intended to play any part in his life at all. Or if I had been marked only to see him playing his.

Maybe in some other life, we would resolve all the unfinished chess games between us. I knew that in this lifetime, I had spent all that I had to give him. And from now on, I would never lie awake on a bitter bed or wake up in the morning with half-forgotten dreams of him clashing with the day's menu.

He sat down next to me. Autumn brown. The smell of burning pines around him.

The seed he had given me was possibly dead. Just like the future we would never share.

I smiled wistfully at the pool. It had come to this. A love that had been my summer and spring. Golden warm. Sap green. Eager. Buried now under layers of scalding ice. Waiting to die. Or to be reborn.

I wondered if we would ever love again. If we were a never-ending story. Divided only by little commas. Inseparable even when separated. But at this moment, I only saw a blue shadow that had once promised me my youth. A man who was my defence against everything. Even himself. A man who was perhaps nothing but an overcoat I had hung on an empty peg to feel less lonely. Maybe he was nothing but my stubborn refusal to grow up. My last scrap of beauty in a world devoid of it.

He watched me. His smile weighing the words he would speak. When he spoke, his voice had no affection, 'I was half-joking when I said all those things last night. It's been so long. I have forgotten how to speak to you. You should never take me seriously. If you want me to apologise, I will.'

I smudged a charcoal leaf with my thumb and said without looking up, 'Apologise for what?'

When I raised my head, he looked slightly flushed. An angry shadow had slashed his forehead in half.

'You don't know what I am talking about?' he spoke with some effort.

'No.'

'I didn't make love to a ghost last night. It was you, wasn't it?' his words were like tightly-packed sardines in a box of cold, frozen rage.

'Was it?'

He watched me. My slim, bare arms with two sliver bangles. My wine-coloured, white-flowered cotton dress. My breasts. My long brown hair falling in small rivulets over my shoulders. The sketch pad resting on my thighs. My intertwined ankles. A body that mocked him. As if it had never been touched.

There was a faint incredulity in his gaze. As if he could not believe the twirl of the pencil between my fingers. Or the way, my foot tapped to a song he could not hear.

'You don't remember that I was in your bed last night?' he watched me with narrow eyes.

He got up and blocked the pool from my gaze, 'I should not have bothered. But I know that you wanted me. Always have. Always will. And you will never forget. Anyway why argue about what is over and done with? These things are part of life. One should get over them and move on. I always do. I don't even remember the last time I saw you.

But you remember, don't you? How many years has it been? Since I saw you last?'

His eyes peered down at me. I saw in them Ma and myself and the bundles of pain and fear we had carried on our backs. I saw strangers ripping apart Ma's life in Lahore. I saw her life-long mourning. I saw the sodden walls of Patiala, Papu's gray body, the cotton tufts in his dead nostrils, boys who left condoms in my letter-box after his death, the false hair pinned on my head at my wedding.

I saw myself on the steps of Annaville shivering with Ma's losses and my pain. I saw Samir taking my life and putting it in a jam bottle he would never open. And then I looked at him, the longest I ever had and said, 'I don't remember.'

Acknowledgements

For many saviours, friends, miracle workers and rainmakers, who nudged, patted, reminded me to keep the dream of this book alive.

Nitin for giving me my first computer and my second and for flagging off this journey. For being family beyond the definitions of family. For everything that cannot be measured or returned.

Aryaman, the handsome little chef, kitten rescuer, pain reliever and stress buster . . . for teaching me (sometimes in vain) how to behave better and to swear less than usual.

Sadhana and Bimal Shukla for creating a life where everyone is welcomed and nurtured and everything smells and feels like home.

Dr Vijay Ahuja for humanity and friendship.

Rosa Kuscharskyj and Teji Sir of the British Co-Ed School Patiala for opening a window in a wall of darkness.

Deepak Agnihotri for tirelessly celebrating life.

Mr B.D. Purohit and late Shivinder Kaur, my teachers at KV, for making me believe.

For Rupa Gulab, my no-nonsense fairy godmother who said to me, exasperated, 'Sign the bloody contract and be a little optimistic, deal?'

Navtej, my long distance life line.

Sheba Thayil for those larger than life WOWS, wide eyes, high heels and deathless conversations.

Superna Thakur, for valiantly rescuing my manuscript from a Delhi publication house where it lay unread for months.

Dr Narendra Pani and Jamuna who told me one crowded day on MG Road, 'Don't look back!'

Kalpana Shah. Thank you for holding my hand when I was learning to walk.

Seetal Iyer. For your ridiculous generosity. For that upright, beautiful spirit and all the wonderful things you don't want to hear about yourself.

Rashme Hegde Gopi for throwing open her heart and her home to me and tirelessly asking, 'So what happened to your book? Nothing? It will.' For Shiva.

To Meera Haran Alva for listening.

Gauri Vij for being Gauri Vij.

Shashi Deshpande who has been gracious even when she did not need to be.

And to dear Deepthi (if I may!) who threw me a life jacket when I needed it most.

And everyone who gave me wings, repaired hope and faith. And those who did not.